ChatGPT-A
English Wr

U0035183

ChatGPT 時代的
英文寫作術

從靈感發想、大綱擬定到完成，
用AI輔助寫作6步驟SOP，輕鬆寫出完美文章

前言
成為世界潮流的 ChatGPT

　　我忘不了 2022 年 12 月初次接觸 ChatGPT 的瞬間。如果您正在使用 ChatGPT，請在 ChatGPT 的輸入欄位直接輸入以下提示詞（prompt）。

Prompt

　Write a 5-paragraph narrative essay about "My First Day of High School."

　　輸入提示詞並且按 Enter 鍵，ChatGPT 就會馬上依照所給的主題（高中的第一天），用完美的英文寫出以五個段落構成的文章。身為教導英文寫作的老師，我最初認為這項新技術是個災難。只要一個點擊就能寫出完美的英文文章，學生還會想要自己實際寫作文嗎？而對於寫作作業，老師能夠分辨學生的文章和 ChatGPT 寫的文章嗎？最重要的是，在這個只要點一點就會跑出一堆資訊的時代，課堂上教學的內容還有什麼用呢？各種想法一個接著一個浮現。事實上，美國許多初中、高中、大學的課堂上禁止使用 ChatGPT 的新聞，也曾經是蔚為一時的話題。

在初次接觸的強烈衝擊過後，我又仔細地思考了一段時間。我突然覺得，ChatGPT 對教師而言，或許不是一場災難，而是一個機會。對學生而言，不也是多了一位 24 小時幫助自己的英語老師嗎？而且，還是會配合自己的實力，提供最個人化的協助的老師。而老師也找到了一位能在課堂上隨時幫助自己教學的最佳授課伙伴，不是嗎？

ChatGPT 已經成為世界潮流。透過 ChatGPT，這個世界正在改變中。曾經看似最難改變的學校課堂，也能感覺到許多變化正在發生。過去教育界未解決的最大課題「依程度區分的個人化學習」，或許有望成為可能。同時，在 AI 時代，也必須重新定義教學與學習的意義。

本書是以 2023 學年第一學期在首爾科學高中用 ChatGPT 輔助的英文寫作（English Writing）教學內容為基礎。書中不僅單純介紹 ChatGPT，也具體介紹 ChatGPT 在英語教學中——尤其是英文寫作的教學——實際應用的方法。另外，我也盡可能收錄了我和學生在課堂上使用過的各種提示詞。我期待這本書能成為眾多教師在英語課堂上應用 ChatGPT 時的實用指南。此外，我也希望讓學習英文寫作的學生知道藉此獲得（而且徹底運用）最佳個人英語教師的方法。在此，我也要對一起上了一學期課程的首爾科學高中第 33 屆、34 屆學生致上深深的謝意。

目錄

請注意

1. 根據 OpenAI 使用條款，ChatGPT 服務使用者必須年滿 13 歲。此外，若使用者未滿 18 歲，需獲得父母或監護人同意才能使用。在課程中使用 ChatGPT 前，請務必獲得父母同意。

2. ChatGPT 生成的資訊需要驗證。ChatGPT 是基於 Transformer 架構而建構的語言模型，它學習了用給予的單字預測下一個單字的過程，雖然功能強大，但也有可能把錯誤的資訊說得像真的一樣，這種情況稱為幻覺（hallucination）。這是因為，就算模型所使用的學習資料沒有相關的資訊，也會試圖用學習過的資訊組織出對於問題的回答。所以，在課堂上使用 ChatGPT 時，一定要意識到 ChatGPT 可能產生錯誤的資訊，因而需要驗證。

3. 書中介紹的 ChatGPT 功能，以及其他應用程式及服務的相關介紹，可能隨著版本更新、功能調整或停止維護而不符合現況，本書無法保證書中所有內容永久有效。

4. 書中出現的人名皆為假名。

關於 ChatGPT 的
幾個疑問

ChatGPT 是什麼？

　　ChatGPT 是 OpenAI 開發的對話型人工智慧模型。ChatGPT 中的 GPT 是「Generative Pre-trained Transformer」的縮寫。G、P、T 的意義分別如下。

G：代表 Generative（生成）。
GPT 是生成式模型，具有依照輸入內容生成新文本的能力。

P：代表 Pre-trained（預訓練）。
GPT 是經過大規模文本資料預先訓練後，再針對特定作業微調（Fine-tuning）過的模型。

T：代表 Transformer（轉換器）。
GPT 是基於 Transformer 架構而建構的。Transformer 透過模仿人類注意力機制的深度學習方式，重新審視重要的部分而進行機器學習。

作為基礎的 Transformer 架構是在 2017 年 Google 發表的〈Attention is All You Need〉[1]這篇論文首次介紹的。如果想進一步了解，請在 Google 直接搜尋這篇論文的標題。要完全理解內容可能很困難，但可以掌握整體模型的樣貌。[2]

ChatGPT 是以 GPT 模型為基礎而建構的對話型人工智慧模型，它會模仿人的對話，並且針對各種問題與狀況生成回答。尤其因為 ChatGPT 學習了大規模的文本資料，所以具備對於各種主題與情境的理解力。例如，它可以應用在日常對話、知識詢問、解決問題、創意工作等各種領域。這個模型透過與使用者對話來進行回答並提供資訊，並且可以在類似的對話情況中持續自然的對話。

不過，由於模型是以事先學習過的資料為基礎來運作，因此對於被賦予的資料範圍以外的知識或最新資訊可能有其侷限。因為是以過去的資料建立，所以可能尚未更新最新資訊。此外，模型自動生成的回答未必總是正確、完美，所以仍然需要使用者的判斷與求證。

1　Ashish Vaswani 等人，〈Attention is All you Need〉，NIPS，2017
2　在 Youtube 上搜尋「Attention is All you Need」，可以找到各種精簡說明這篇論文的影片，有興趣的讀者可以看看。

如何開始使用 ChatGPT

　　請上 http://chat.openai.com/，按畫面上的「註冊」按鈕後註冊帳戶即可。

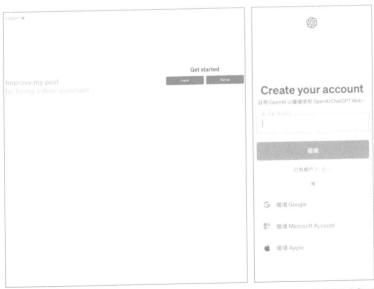

ChatGPT 註冊帳戶畫面

如何與 ChatGPT 溝通

非常簡單！只要在畫面下方的訊息輸入框輸入提示詞
（prompt），按 Enter 鍵即可。ChatGPT 有記住過去對話的

ChatGPT 提示詞輸入畫面

能力，所以也可以在相同情境下連續提出問題。如果想要
開始全新的對話，只要按左上角的按鈕開始新交談即可。
本書出版時的免費版本為 GPT-3.5 模型。如果每月支付 20
美元升級 GPT Plus，就可以完整使用更先進的 GPT-4 模
型。本書使用的是可以免費利用的 GPT-3.5 模型。如果你
預計經常使用 ChatGPT，也想利用更快、更進步的功能，
就可以考慮使用付費版本。

　　提示詞是對 ChatGPT 提出的問題。你可以像是跟
身旁的朋友對話一般來寫。在正式開始之前，可以先跟
ChatGPT 打招呼，培養一下感情。請在輸入框輸入以下的
內容看看。

Prompt

👤　Hello? Who are you? 哈囉，你是誰？

🌀　Hello! I'm ChatGPT, an AI language model
developed by OpenAI. I'm here to provide information,
answer questions, and assist with various topics you
might need help with. How can I assist you today?

哈囉！我是 ChatGPT，是由 OpenAI 開發的 AI 語言模型。我在這裡提供資訊、回答問題，並協助您可能需要幫助的各種主題。我今天可以怎麼協助您呢？

　　如果用英文對 ChatGPT 提問，會得到英文回答，而用中文詢問就會得到中文回答。很聰明吧？但請記得，因為預訓練的文本大部分是英文，所以用英文提問，會比用中文提問獲得更仔細且正確的答案。此外，即使問的是類似的內容，也可能因為使用的提示詞（prompt）不同，而產生不同的結果。所以，寫出好的提示詞（提出好的問題）是最重要的。

如何寫出好的提示詞

使用 ChatGPT 時，要寫出好的提示詞，有以下幾個原則。

1. 明確而具體地表達

在提示詞中明確地表示自己的請求或問題。提示詞越具體、越簡潔，得到相關答案的可能性就越高。請避免提出模糊或者範圍太廣的提示詞。

Example Can you provide me with a brief summary of the key features of the latest iPhone model?

你可以提供我最新 iPhone 型號主要功能的簡略概要嗎？

2. 提供情境

當問題或要求需要背景資訊或情境時,請將這些資訊包括在提示詞中。這樣有助於 ChatGPT 理解情境,提供更正確且符合需求的回答。

Example　I'm planning a trip to Tokyo next month. Could you suggest some popular tourist attractions and best places to eat in the city?

我正在計畫下個月去東京的旅行。你可以推薦東京的一些人氣旅遊景點與最佳餐廳嗎?

3. 指定想要的形式

如果對於回答的類型或形式有基本的設定,請在提示詞中提及。這樣有助於模型生成比較合適的回答。

Example　Please list three advantages and two disadvantages of using solar energy for residential purposes.

請列出使用住宅用太陽能的三個優點與兩個缺點。

4. 要求模型分步驟思考或討論優缺點

如果希望 ChatGPT 透過問題進行推論，或者考慮其他觀點，請明確地要求它針對特定主題分步驟思考或提出贊成與反對的論據。

(Example) Can you outline the steps involved in setting up a personal budget? Please explain each step in detail.

你可以概述建立個人預算的步驟嗎？請詳細說明每個步驟。

5. 設定情境或角色（賦予角色）

要讓對話更有趣，你可以指定 ChatGPT 要採用的情境或角色。可以是想像的人物、特定領域的專家，或者其他覺得適合的角色。

(Example) Imagine you are a historian specializing in World War II. Can you provide insights into the major events that led to the Allied victory?

想像你是專門研究第二次世界大戰的歷史學家。關於致使同盟國勝利的主要事件，你可以提供一些洞見嗎？

(Example) I want you to act as an English teacher and give me feedback to improve my essay.

我要你扮演英語老師，並且給我回饋意見來改善我的短文。

Tip

請務必記得，要對 ChatGPT 使用明確且具體的提示詞，提供指定的情境與形式，並且賦予角色，才能得到最好的結果。

有助於英語學習的
ChatGPT 相關擴充應用程式介紹

※ 書中介紹的程式與服務，可能不完全符合現況，敬請留意。

在 Chrome 瀏覽器的線上應用程式商店，可以找到針對 ChatGPT 的擴充應用程式，增加使用者自訂命令詞或其他額外功能。透過擴充功能，可以更容易地使用 ChatGPT 的各種功能。以下介紹對於學習英語最有用的擴充應用程式。

1. AIPRM

AIPRM

如果希望從 ChatGPT 得到好的結果，就必須輸入好的提示詞。但在一開始就寫出高水準的提示詞絕非易事。要在特定情境中寫出好的提示詞，必須有相關領域的專門知識，也要熟悉「提示工程」（prompt engineering）。

AIPRM 收集了專家製作的提示詞，讓使用者容易取用。即使是初學者，也可以輕鬆應用專家生成、驗證過的提示詞。就像其他擴充程式一樣，只要在 Google Chrome 瀏覽器的線上應用程式商店輸入 AIPRM，就可以加到 Chrome 使用。

　　成功安裝 AIPRM 之後，請在搜尋欄位輸入「English」或「Learning English」、「English Essay」等關鍵詞。你將看到許多由專家製作、令人驚豔的提示詞。我個人覺得「Essay Grader」這組提示詞非常神奇，也很喜歡。將作文置入這組提示詞，就可以自動評分並顯示理由。雖然不能完全依賴它對作文的評價，但還是可以用輕鬆的心情，讓程式評價自己的文章看看。關於作文的評價與評分，之後會更詳細探討。

2. Talk-To-ChatGPT

VoiceWave: ChatGPT Voice Control

Talk-To-ChatGPT

　　另一個要了解的擴充應用程式是 VoiceWave: ChatGPT Voice Control。ChatGPT 雖然已經加入了發音功能，但無法配合口說與聽力練習的需求微調語音。VoiceWave 使用聲音辨識與文字轉語音技術，所以用麥克風就可以跟 ChatGPT

對話，也能聽到回答的語音，而且能調整語速。只要在 Google Chrome 的線上應用程式商店搜尋 VoiceWave: ChatGPT Voice Control 並加入瀏覽器就可以使用。

成功安裝之後，打開 ChatGPT 首頁時就會在輸入框旁邊看到麥克風按鈕，準備好麥克風之後，按下按鈕就可以開始用語音輸入文字。

用語音輸入文字

而如果點擊視窗右上角的拼圖圖示、點擊「ChatGPT 的語音控制」，再點擊右上角的齒輪圖示，就可以設定語言與文字轉語音（TTS）的聲音與速度等等。對於想要利用 ChatGPT 來練習英語聽力與口說的人，很推薦使用看看。

文字轉語音設定

對於英文寫作教學特別有用的
人工智慧工具

1. Grammarly

Grammarly 畫面

　　Grammarly[3] 是以人工智慧為基礎,用來修正英文作文與文法的線上校對工具。它可以分析使用者的作文,辨識出文法錯誤、拼字錯誤、風格與表達方式可以改善的事

3　https://www.grammarly.com

項，並給予建議。在我們英文寫作的課堂上，會在寫作的最後階段利用 Grammarly 程式。

2. Quillbot

Quillbot 畫面

Quillbot[4] 是以人工智慧為基礎的寫作工具，會以各種方式重新建構句子，對於產生更好的句子很有幫助。而且，Quillbot 也能將輸入的句子變得更流暢（Fluency）、更正式（Formal）、更簡單（Simple）、更長（Expand），或者更有創意（Creative）。如此一來，就能在維持原文意義的同時，將作文的風格改得更多元而豐富。另外，它也能協助分析使用者輸入的句子或段落，並建議有意義、文法上正確的替代句子，進而改善作文內容。

4 https://quillbot.com

3. DeepL

DeepL 畫面

DeepL[5] 是 2017 年問世、以人工智慧為基礎的機器翻譯服務，能夠在指定語言間進行快速且正確的翻譯。DeepL 使用大量語言資料與神經網路（Neural Network）在句子層面進行翻譯，並且在理解翻譯的情境後產生自然的翻譯。本書出版時，DeepL 已經支援 31 種語言的翻譯，除了主要的歐洲語言以外，也能翻譯中文、日文、韓文等各種語言。在我個人使用到目前為止的翻譯服務中，DeepL 應該是功能最優秀的，我在需要翻譯時也很常用。本書所有英中翻譯也都是由 DeepL 輔助進行的。

---

5 https://www.deepl.com

第2章

開始用 ChatGPT
輔助英文寫作教學

ChatGPT 時代
英文寫作教學的意義

　　20 年前，微軟的 Word 開始內建拼字檢查功能。這在當時是非常革命性的。但同時，許多老師也擔心這項革命性功能的副作用。他們擔心學生太依賴拼字檢查功能，不花心思輸入正確的拼字。甚至有些老師說，這種功能應該視為「作弊」。

　　但現在呢？曾經被懷疑是作弊工具的這項智慧功能，現在已經成為寫出高完成度文章的必備工具了。事實上，對線上文法檢查工具的研究顯示，文法檢查功能可以為學生提供文法方面的即時回饋，而學生也會接收到這個回饋。[6] 換句話說，學生並非（像許多老師擔心的那樣）完全不思考、只是點擊「拼字檢查」而已，而是透過回饋而實際進行學習。

　　我們（包含老師與學生）已經在寫作時使用 AI 了。前

6　Yang Hyejin，〈Efficiency of Online Grammar Checker in English Writing Performance and Students' Perceptions〉，淑明女子大學，2018。

面提到的拼字檢查軟體也是以機器學習與模式識別之類的 AI 技術為基礎。這種功能最近與深度學習及自然語言處理技術等令人矚目的發展結合，變得更加精細化。現在已經超越了單純找出錯字的程度，而達到了能找出情境方面誤用單字的水準。

再看看另一個例子吧。雖然我們可能沒有意識到，但 Google 的自動完成功能也在協助我們寫作。請想想看在 Google 用英文搜尋資料的時候。即使只輸入幾個我們想找的關鍵詞，Google 也會透過自動完成功能大幅縮小搜尋範圍。而在 Gmail 寫信的時候，Google 也能依照已經寫出來的單字預測後面會出現的單字，並且自動建議最好的表達方式。

事實上，學生現在已經透過 Google 翻譯、Naver Papago、DeepL、Quillbot、Grammarly 等等，在整個寫作過程中積極利用更先進的 AI。許多曾被視為作弊行為的智慧型學習工具，現在正在為學生的整個寫作過程注入許多活力。

不過，各位讀者可能會反問，在課堂上使用拼字檢查軟體，跟使用 ChatGPT 不是完全不同的兩回事嗎？是的，沒錯。因為 ChatGPT 會「生成」全新的內容。ChatGPT 是以（運用各種階層的神經網路）模仿人類頭腦的深度學習演算法為基礎的技術。它學習了大量的資料集，預測沒有明確編寫為程式的事情，還能生成新的想法與文章。

和 ChatGPT 對話時會覺得像在跟人類對話，也正是因為這個原因。所以，在這個時刻，我們必須更深入思考將 ChatGPT 當成寫作學習工具來使用的方法。我們從兩個層面來看。

第一個層面
擺脫恐懼與只能二選一的觀念
——採用混合方式

首先，我們必須先擺脫擔心 AI 工具入侵寫作課堂，可能使學生寫作能力明顯惡化的恐懼。儘管寫作過程或方式可能隨著時代更迭而有所變化，但寫作行為本身並不會消失。現在寫著書的我正坐在電腦前，雖然不像過去一樣使用紙和筆，但一樣「在寫作」的事實是不變的。我們只要更善用先進的工具就行了。

此外，我們也必須擺脫在完全相反的兩種立場中（「在課堂上必須完全允許 AI 工具」以及「在課堂上必須完全禁止 AI」的立場）只允許二選一的作法。我們必須採取的作法是，在授課時有智慧地使用 AI、提升學習者的學習效果，同時也更注重 AI 不具備的人性要素。我們將這個作法稱為人類－AI 混合方式（Blended Approach）。學生透過 ChatGPT 等 AI 工具創造新的構想，或以 ChatGPT 的生成內容為出發點，結合自己的構想後，產出更優秀的成品。如此一來，了解聰明地使用 AI 的方式，就更加重要了。我們必須正確認知到 AI 展現其優點的領域，並且在特定情境中積極尋求 AI 的協助。但我們也必須知道一項事實，那就是在需要人類的感性、創意與打動人心的口吻的學習空間，必須在人工智慧之上添加人類智慧。也就是說，我們在課堂上必須靈活地遊走於人類智慧與人工智慧之間。

第二個層面

我們應該允許什麼，
又不該允許什麼？

　　在寫作課實際應用強調人類與 AI 間靈活互動的混合方式時，必然會遇到這個問題：我們應該允許什麼，又不該允許什麼？換句話說，我們必須深思，在寫作過程中應該容許使用 ChatGPT 之類的 AI 工具到什麼程度。其實這也是這學期我在英文寫作課程採用 ChatGPT 時最苦惱的。

　　在此我想介紹《教科書消失的教室》[7] 這本書的作者麥特・米勒提出的標準。首先，米勒強調將 AI 與教育結合時，必須要有明確判斷容許與不容許之處的標準。而為了制定這樣的標準，他也依照在課堂上使用 AI 工具的程度不

7　Matt Miller，《教科書消失的教室》（韓譯版，原標題：*Ditch That Textbook*），Bang Hyunjin 譯，Jisikframe 出版，2018

同，列出了界定作弊與抄襲的判斷標準光譜。各位讀者認為以下六個項目[8]中，到哪個項目為止算是作弊或抄襲呢？

① 學生透過 AI 用提示詞生成回答，直接複製後交給老師。
② 學生閱讀用 AI 生成的回答，修改、調整後提交。
③ 學生用 AI 生成多個回答，運用其中最好的部分並編輯後提交。
④ 學生寫下主要想法，讓 AI 以此為基礎生成草稿，並提供幫助改善的回饋意見。
⑤ 學生參考網路／AI，獲得想法後自己寫作並提交。
⑥ 學生所有的作業都不詢問 AI 或網路，而是自己寫。

根據米勒的定義，作弊通常是指學生為了取得不當利益，偽裝自身理解或能力的不誠實行為。抄襲則是指將並非自身作品的某作品當成自己創作的情況。不過，對於這個問題的回答，比起詞語的定義，我們或許更大程度依賴自己對「作弊」或「抄襲」的直觀感受。

首先是將 ChatGPT 所寫的文章直接提交的情況。直觀上，這顯然可以視為作弊或抄襲。但如果學生是讀了透過 ChatGPT 生成的文章，並且修改、編輯後提交，這可以說是作弊或抄襲嗎？事實上，這個問題的答案不但隨著每個老師而不同，也會隨著寫作作業的類型而不同。

---

8 Matt Miller, <ChatGPT, Chatbots and Artificial Intelligence in Education>, 2022.12.17, https://ditchthattextbook.com/ai/#tve-jump-18606008967

例如，試想一下在部落格介紹自己喜愛歌手的情況。我認為將 ChatGPT 針對這位歌手寫的各種文章用自己的觀點修改、編輯並完成一篇文章，也不是什麼壞事。但如果是要寫出表達自身主張的五段作文呢？如果用 ChatGPT 生成的幾篇文章來拼湊，肯定會有問題。所以，在寫作時可以容許使用 AI 到什麼程度（或者要不要在自己的寫作中運用），可能隨著作業類型而各有不同。

這樣的話，在我們撰寫英文作文的課堂上，又應該容許使用 AI 到什麼程度呢？事實上，雖然可能隨著文章的類型而稍有不同，但我在課堂上選擇了「學生自己產出主要構想，由 AI 以此為基礎，提供幫助改善的回饋意見」這種方式。尤其在撰寫記敘文（Narrative Essay）時，構想的獨創性特別重要，因為沒有自身個性的文章，只要換個名字，也能說是其他任何人的文章。文章必須以自己最個人化的想法為出發點。然後，我們才能在這個基礎上接受各種 AI 工具的協助。

ChatGPT 之類的 AI 工具，什麼時候是學習工具，什麼時候又是作弊行為，並沒有絕對的標準。但重要的是，我們必須在各種寫作情境中不斷思考這個問題。我們也應該透過問這樣的問題，對於要在寫作中使用多少 AI，與參與學習過程的人員取得共識。

運用 ChatGPT 的英文寫作過程

現在讓我們大略看看，在英文作文寫作過程中如何進行人類－AI 混合的學習。

寫作前的過程

產生構想、組織構想、確定構想

首先，學生可以透過 ChatGPT 獲得符合各種文類的寫作主題推薦。藉由以下的提示詞，你可以查看適合各文類的各種主題。請在底線部分填入 Narrative Essay（記敘文）、Descriptive Essay（描述文）、Expository Essay（說明文）、Argumentative Essay（論說文）等各種文類看看。關於各種文類，之後會正式討論。

Recommend me good topics for a compare and contrast essay.

推薦我對比文的好主題。

　　決定主題後，學生可以就相關主題對 ChatGPT 提出各種問題並累積背景知識。這個階段的重點，是掌握自己對於主題已經知道什麼，以及還需要進一步了解什麼。在 ChatGPT 的時代，重要的不是擁有許多知識（在知識方面，ChatGPT 擁有更多），而是正確了解自己想要什麼、不知道什麼，以及為了補足自己不知道的事而提出好問題。這裡舉個例子。假設有位對歷史感興趣的學生，決定要寫第一次與第二次世界大戰的對比文，就可以像下面一樣要求提供關於對比文的構想。

I am going to write a compare and contrast essay about World War I vs. World War II: Explore the causes, impact, and outcomes of these two major global conflicts. I want you to brainstorm ideas for this essay.

我要寫一篇關於第一次與第二次世界大戰的對比文：
探討這兩次重大全球衝突的起因、影響和結果。我希
望你為這篇文章腦力激盪出一些構想。

如果 ChatGPT 提供的資訊有自己不了解的部分，可以
像下面一樣要求額外說明。

Prompt

Can you explain more about 'Rise of fascism and
totalitarian ideologies' in Europe?

可以進一步說明歐洲「法西斯主義與極權主義意識形
態的興起」嗎？

學生可以針對主題想出適當的問題，並輸入 ChatGPT
尋找答案，用這樣的方式增加與主題有關的背景知識。藉
此，可以拓展並完善自己的構想，使它成為寫作的素材。
這裡要再次強調的是，在人類－AI 混合方式中，學生必須
具備的最重要能力，是提出好問題的能力。

寫作時的過程
撰寫大綱、修正與編輯

經過探索主題的階段後，在正式寫作的階段也可以接受 ChatGPT 的協助。我們也能將與 ChatGPT 溝通而得到的構想作為基礎，要求提出寫作文章的大綱（Outline）。當然，如果不滿意 ChatGPT 生成的大綱，可以不斷要求修改。

Prompt

I am writing a 5-paragraph expository essay about World War I vs. World War II: Explore the causes, impact, and outcomes of these two major global conflicts. I want you to write an essay outline. Each body paragraph contains the contrasts of the causes, impact, and outcomes of two World Wars.

我正在寫關於第一次與第二次世界大戰的五段說明文：探討這兩次重大全球衝突的起因、影響和結果。請寫出一份文章大綱。各個正文段落包括兩次世界大戰起因、影響和結果的對比。

此外，實際寫作後（寫下草稿後），學生除了找同學或老師以外，也可以向 ChatGPT 尋求回饋意見。在 ChatGPT 的提示詞輸入欄位直接貼上文章，並且使用各種提示詞，就可以要求具體的回饋意見。可以要求修正成符合文法的文章，或者透過選擇多樣化的單字來提高文章的生動感。此外，也可以要求用連接詞使文章更有凝聚力，或者要求改變氣氛，把文章變得比較正式或流暢。請看以下提示詞。這裡列出的提示詞都是我們在英文寫作課實際使用過的。關於提示詞的詳細內容，之後會更詳細討論。

Prompt

Make the paragraph visually clear.

讓段落在視覺描寫方面變得清晰。

Prompt

Fix grammar errors or change words to more vivid and complicated ones.

修正文法錯誤，或把單字換成比較生動、複雜的。

Prompt

Make the paragraph below more effective while unchanging the story.

在不改變故事情節的情況下，使下面的段落更有效果。

Prompt

Find grammatical errors in the following paragraph, and improve my paragraph.

在以下段落中找出文法錯誤，並改善我的段落。

Prompt

Can you make the sentences seem more connected for the paragraph below?

你能讓下面段落的句子看起來更連貫嗎？

Prompt

Can you make my descriptive paragraph more interesting, connecting the sentences more naturally?

你能讓我的描述段落更有趣，並且更自然地連接句子嗎？

How can I make my argumentation better?

我該如何改善我的論證？

What are some changes I could do to make the essay flow more smoothly?

我可以做哪些改變，使這篇文章更流暢？

　　這裡最該注意的是，是否將 ChatGPT 的回饋意見實際應用在自己的文章上，最終仍取決於寫文章的作者本人。不可能只靠一個提示詞，就像魔法一般把文章變得完美。將 ChatGPT 生成的各種回饋意見運用在自己的文章、進行取捨的能力，終究是必要的。

　　到了這裡，我們已經簡單了解了 ChatGPT 時代的寫作與人類－AI 混合方式。就像現在用電腦而不是紙筆寫作已經理所當然一般，在不久的將來，用 ChatGPT 之類的 AI 工具寫作也會變成很自然的事。而為了因應這樣的時代，英文寫作教學也必須不斷改變。現在就正式開始教學的部分吧。

第3章

用 ChatGPT 輔助
英文寫作

用 ChatGPT
輔助段落寫作

　　怎樣才能寫出好的英文文章？這實在是很難的問題，也是我在教英文寫作時最常被學生問到的問題。那麼，我們稍微縮小問題的範圍，限定在短文寫作。怎樣才能寫出好的英文短文？短文是由幾個段落構成的（大部分的短文由五、六個段落組成），所以寫好英文的段落十分重要。於是大家會接著問：怎樣才能把段落寫好呢？要寫好段落，當然就要寫出好的句子，並且把句子放在適當的地方。我們的英文寫作課從段落寫作開始，因為好作文是從好句子所組成的好段落開始的。現在我們要稍微探討段落是什麼，並且實際寫一段看看。

段落的定義、特徵與構成要素

段落究竟是指什麼？下面就問 ChatGPT 看看。

Prompt

👤 段落是什麼？

🌀 所謂段落，是指與一個核心想法或主題有關的多個句子所構成的文章寫作單位。好的段落大多由主題句、闡述說明句與結論句構成。主題句介紹段落的主要想法，闡述說明句在主題句後面補充詳細資訊、例子或說明。結論句則會總結段落的核心內容，或者銜接下一段。好的段落對於從短文到電子郵件的各種文章寫作都很重要，也有助於有邏輯並有一貫性地傳達資訊。

如同我們在 ChatGPT 的回答所見，段落是寫作時組成的邏輯性結構與意義單位，是文本中最基本的單位。段落一般而言處理一個主題或想法，並且由和主題相關的一些句子組成。在英文寫作課的第一個小時，我們通常會先掌握段落的概念與特性，並且了解構成段落的各種要素。在

這裡，首先要進一步了解一下段落的特性。在 ChatGPT 輸入以下提示詞看看。

請告訴我段落的特徵。

段落具有以下特徵：

1. 統一性（Unity）：段落應該聚焦於一個主題或想法上，而其中的句子應該與此想法有關。

2. 連貫性（Coherence）：段落內的句子之間應該有邏輯關聯，並明確地傳達一個主題。

3. 主題句（Topic Sentence）：好的段落應該以明確而簡潔的主題句開始。它也應該說明段落的核心想法。

4. 闡述說明句（Supporting Sentences）：主題句應該要有多個句子將其具體化，並提供例子、詳細資訊、說明等。

5. 轉折詞或片語（Transition Words or Phrases）：應該用轉折詞或片語使句子之間的銜接流暢。它們扮演顯示句子間關係的角色。

6. 長度（Length）：段落雖然應該具備足以傳達想法的長度，但不應過長，否則可能使讀者注意力渙散或感到混亂。

7. 連貫性（Consistency）：段落的語氣與風格應該連貫，如果出現新的想法或主題，應該在新的段落介紹。

　　ChatGPT 用七個關鍵詞告訴我們段落具備的特性。這裡還要補充的是，區分段落最具代表性的形式是首行縮排。通常可以用空白鍵空幾格，或者按鍵盤上的 Tab 鍵縮排七個空格的距離。此外，段落長度以五到七句為宜。太短不足以傳達段落的內容，太長則會讓讀者注意力下降。

　　段落中最重要的句子叫做主題句（Topic Sentence），一般而言通常會以主題句作為第一個句子來開啟段落，讀者可以從這個句子掌握到段落的核心內容。段落的最後一句則通常以結論句（Concluding Sentence）結尾。結論句的作用是為段落的整體內容收尾，並且向讀者強調最後要傳達的訊息。它讓讀者回想起段落內容的主旨，也能強調段落的目的，並且更明確地傳達希望讀者得到的資訊。精心撰寫的結論句，對於提高文章完成度而言扮演重要角色。

段落的結構
主題句 ⇩ **和主題有關的詳細事實或資訊** ⇩ **結論句**

　　如上圖所示，段落由多個句子組成，大致上分為主題句→支持中心思想或使其具體化的詳細事實或資訊→結論句。接下來，我們再用 ChatGPT 進一步了解段落中的各種構成要素。先用它生成一個段落。

Prompt

👤 Write a narrative paragraph about 'Spring and coffee'.

　　寫一個關於「春天與咖啡」的記敘段落。

　　我用這個提示詞請它以「春天與咖啡」為主題寫一個記敘段落（Narrative Paragraph）[9]，因為現在正是風光明媚的春天，而我坐在咖啡廳、喝著咖啡寫這篇文章。真期待 ChatGPT 會寫出怎樣的文章。

9　記敘段落傳達作者自己的故事，或者展現個人經驗。其他寫作類型還有描述段落、說明段落、主張段落等。

Spring and coffee are a perfect match. There's something about the warm sunshine and the fresh, crisp air that makes a cup of coffee taste even better. I love to sit outside on a quiet morning, with a book in hand and a steaming cup of coffee on the table in front of me. As I take a sip, I can feel the warmth spreading throughout my body, and I feel invigorated and ready to start the day. The aroma of the coffee blends with the sweet fragrance of blooming flowers, creating a sensory experience that is both calming and energizing. Even as the day warms up and the sun gets stronger, a cup of iced coffee provides the perfect refreshing pick-me-up. **Spring and coffee go hand in hand, and I can't imagine one without the other.**

春天和咖啡是絕配。和煦的陽光和清新的空氣有種讓一杯咖啡更美味的能力。我喜歡在寧靜的早晨坐在室外，手捧一本書，面前的桌上放著一杯熱氣騰騰的咖啡。當我啜飲一口時，我能感覺到溫暖傳遍全身，我感到精神振奮，準備開始新的一天。咖啡的香氣與盛開的鮮花的甜香交織在一起，給人一種既平靜又充滿活力的感官體驗。即使天氣逐漸轉暖，陽光越來越強烈，一杯冰咖啡也能帶來完美的提神效果。春天與咖啡相得益彰，我無法想像兩者缺一。[10]

---

10 英翻中部分利用 deepl.com 輔助進行。

輸入提示詞之後，ChatGPT 馬上就寫出關於「春天與咖啡」、包含個人感想的記敘段落。第一個句子是顯示段落整體內容核心的主題句，而最後一個句子則是總結段落整體的結論句。它用很好的主題句來表達段落的核心概念，主題句之後的句子也充分呈現了與春天及咖啡相關的個人經驗，而最後的結論句也對這個段落做了很好的總結，可以說是很出色的段落。真厲害！

　　接下來就練習用 ChatGPT 進行段落主題句與結論句的寫作。我刪掉前面那段文字的第一個句子，也就是主題句，並且加入下面的提示語。

Prompt

👤 Write a brief and good topic sentence for the paragraph below.

為下面的段落寫一個簡短又好的主題句。

_____. There's something about the warm sunshine and the fresh, crisp air that makes a cup of coffee taste even better. I love to sit outside on a quiet morning, with a book in hand and a steaming cup of coffee on the table in front of me. As I take a sip, I can feel the warmth spreading throughout my body, and I feel invigorated and ready to start the day. The aroma of the coffee blends with the sweet fragrance of blooming flowers, creating a sensory experience that is both calming and energizing. Even as the day warms up and the sun gets stronger, a cup of iced coffee provides the perfect refreshing pick-me-up. Spring and coffee go hand in hand, and I can't imagine one without the other.

ChatGPT 的回應結果如下。

Topic sentence: The invigorating combination of spring weather and coffee creates a sensory experience that rejuvenates the mind and body.

主題句：春季天氣與咖啡這令人精神煥發的組合，創造出恢復身心活力的感官體驗。

這比之前的主題句「Spring and coffee are a perfect match.」稍微長一點，但清楚寫出了春天與咖啡間的關係這個段落核心概念。下面則是把段落最後的結論句去掉，請 ChatGPT 寫出結論句。

Write a simple and good concluding sentence for the paragraph below.

為下面的段落寫一個簡單又好的結論句。

Spring and coffee are a perfect match. There's something about the warm sunshine and the fresh, crisp air that makes a cup of coffee taste even better. I love to sit outside on a quiet morning, with a book in hand and a steaming cup of coffee on the table in front of me. As I take a sip, I can feel the warmth spreading throughout my body, and I feel invigorated and ready to start the day. The aroma of the coffee blends with the sweet fragrance of blooming flowers, creating a sensory experience that is both calming and energizing. Even as the day warms up and the sun gets stronger, a cup of iced coffee provides the perfect refreshing pick-me-up.

_____.

Concluding sentence: In essence, a perfect spring day is incomplete without a warm cup of coffee to savor and enjoy the beauty of nature.

結論句：總之，沒有一杯溫暖的咖啡來品味並享受大自然的美景，完美的春日就不完整。

　　ChatGPT 寫出了上面這個很棒的結論句，為關於春天與咖啡的段落下了很好的結論。我們可以像這樣透過 ChatGPT 學到段落是什麼，以及如何寫出構成段落的要素。接下來我們要自己寫段落，並且看看如何透過 ChatGPT 得到回饋意見。

用 ChatGPT 書寫段落並獲得回饋意見

到目前為止，我們利用 ChatGPT 詳細探討了段落的定義、特徵與構成要素，而接下來就輪到我們了。我們也用下面提到的主題寫一個段落看看吧？第一個題目是，用一個記敘段落（Narrative Paragraph）寫出自己人生中印象最深的回憶或事件。在寫之前請務必記得，段落是針對一個主題所寫的，並且以主題句＋關於主題的詳細資訊＋結論句組成。

題目1　Write a narrative paragraph about a personal experience that you might characterize as the most amusing, sad, terrifying, satisfying, stupid or rewarding thing you have done or witnessed.

寫一個關於個人經驗的記敘段落，講述你所做過或目睹過最有趣、最悲傷、最恐怖、最令人滿意、最愚蠢或最有價值的一件事。

下面是課堂上學生實際交出的文章。

The trip to Barcelona totally changed my view about architecture. I went to Barcelona 5 years ago with my family. I experienced lots of new things such as delicious Spanish food, tango, and old museums. But the one thing that made me really shocked was the architects in Barcelona, especially which designed by Gaudi. One day I went to park Guell, named after the sponsor of Gaudi. When I first saw the shape and the color of park mixed with the spotlight of Spanish sunlight, I just couldn't say a word. Since I was born and raised in Seoul, the only buildings that I can see in my real life are rectangular-gray-boring-buildings. So colorful and organic form of the park Guell made me speechless. I enjoyed the space itself that I even forgot to take pictures. It was so shocking and enjoyable experience that for a long time after I came back to Korea, I wanted to go back there just for the park Guell.

巴塞隆納之行徹底改變了我對建築的看法。5 年前，我和家人一起去了巴塞隆納。我體驗了很多新事物，比如美味的西班牙食物、探戈舞和古老的博物館。但最讓我震驚的是巴塞隆納的建築師，尤其是高第所設計的。有一天，我去了以高第贊助人的名字命名的奎爾公園。當我第一次看到公園的形狀和顏色與西班牙陽光的照耀混合時，我簡直說不出話來。因為我生長在首爾，現實生活中能看到的建築都是長方形的、灰色的、無聊的建築。所以，奎爾公園豐富多彩的有機形態讓我說不出話來。我很享受那個空間本身，甚至忘記要拍照。如此震撼和愉悅的體驗，讓我在回到韓國後的很長一段時間裡，都想再回到那裡，只為了奎爾公園。

　　學生用一個記敘段落，對於自己拜訪巴塞隆納、看到當地建築物而感到驚豔的經歷做了不錯的敘述。ChatGPT認為學生寫的段落如何呢？試著輸入以下內容。

Prompt

👤 Give me some feedback on my narrative paragraph.

針對我的記敘段落，給我一些回饋意見。

Your narrative paragraph is well written and effectively conveys your experience of how the trip to Barcelona changed your perspective on architecture. You clearly describe the different experiences you had in Barcelona, such as trying new foods and visiting museums, but the focus of the paragraph is on how the architecture you encountered there impacted you.

Your description of visiting Park Guell is particularly effective in conveying your emotions and reactions to the organic and colorful forms of Gaudi's architecture. The way you describe being speechless and forgetting to take pictures effectively conveys how the experience impacted you on a personal level.

One suggestion to improve the paragraph would be to include more sensory details to help the reader fully visualize the experience. For example, you could describe the smells and sounds of Barcelona or the feel of the Spanish sunlight on your skin. Overall, however, your narrative paragraph effectively conveys your personal experience and the impact it had on you.

你的記敘段落寫得很好，有效地傳達了你的經歷，也就是巴塞隆納之行如何改變了你對建築的看法。你清楚地描述了你在巴塞隆納的不同經歷，如嘗試新食物和參觀博物館，但這個段落的重點是你在那裡遇到的建築如何影響了你。

你對於參觀奎爾公園的描述，特別有效地傳達了你對高第建築有機且多彩形式的情感與反應。你描述自己說不出話並且忘記拍照，有效地表達了這次經歷如何在個人層面影響了你。

改進這個段落的一個建議是包含更多感官細節，幫助讀者充分想像這段經歷。例如，你可以描述巴塞隆納的氣味和聲音，或者西班牙陽光照在皮膚上的感覺。不過，整體來說，你的記敘段落有效地傳達了你的個人經歷，以及它對你的影響。

ChatGPT 的評價認為，上面的記敘段落整體而言很優秀。另外也給予回饋意見，建議增加一些感官細節，藉此更有效地傳達個人經驗。我們再嘗試要求更詳細的回饋意見吧？這次讓 ChatGPT 扮演英語老師的角色（還記得前面提過，要寫出好的提示詞，其中一項原則是賦予角色嗎？），請它提供著重於文法與描寫的具體回饋意見。

Now you will become an English teacher and help me to improve the quality of my grammar and mainly improve my adjectives. Every time I send you a text, you will try to give me a way to improve it.

me: <text>

you: <analyze the text and give recommendations>

現在，你將成為一名英語教師，幫我改善我的文法品質，主要是改善我的形容詞。每當我傳送訊息給你的時候，你會努力給我一個改善的方法。

我：〈文本〉

你：〈分析文本並給出建議〉

Great job on describing your experience in Barcelona! Here are some suggestions for improving your text:

- Adjectives: Use more vivid and descriptive adjectives to paint a clearer picture of your experience. For example, instead of just saying "delicious Spanish food," you could say "mouthwatering paella" or "flavorful tapas." Similarly, instead of "old museums," you could say "historic museums filled with ancient artifacts."

- Sentence structure: Vary your sentence structure to keep the reader engaged. Instead of always starting with "I," try starting with a descriptive phrase or using a conjunction to connect two related ideas. For example, you could say "Amidst the tango and historic museums of Barcelona, it was the architects, especially those who designed Gaudi's masterpieces, that left me speechless."

- Grammar: Make sure your verb tenses and subject-verb agreements are correct. For example, instead of saying "the architects in Barcelona, especially which designed by Gaudi," you could say "the architectures in Barcelona, especially which were designed by Gaudi."

- Word choice: Consider using more specific vocabulary to add nuance to your writing. For example, instead of "shocking," you could say "awe-inspiring" or "breathtaking."

Overall, great start!

你把自己在巴塞隆納的經歷描述得很好！以下是改善你的文章的一些建議：

－形容詞：使用比較生動、描述性較強的形容詞，更清晰地描繪你的經歷。例如，不要只說「美味的西班牙食物」，可以說「令人垂涎欲滴的西班牙燉飯」或「滋味豐富的小菜」。同樣地，與其說「古老的博物館」，不如說「充滿古代文物、歷史悠久的博物館」。

－句子結構：變換句子結構以持續吸引讀者。不要總是以「我」開頭，可以嘗試以敘述性片語開頭，或者使用連接詞來連接兩個相關的想法。例如，你可以說：「在探戈和巴塞隆納歷史悠久的博物館等事物之中，讓我說不出話來的是建築師，尤其是設計了高第的傑作的建築師。」

－文法：確保動詞時態與主詞－動詞一致性正確。例如，不要說「巴塞隆納的建築師，尤其是高第所設計的」，而可以說「巴塞隆納的建築物，尤其是高第所設計的」。

－措詞：考慮使用更具體的詞彙為你的文章增加細微差別。例如，你可以說「令人敬畏的」或「令人嘆為觀止的」，而不是「令人震驚的」。

整體而言，這是很好的開始！

接下來，我們要取得對於段落構成要素的詳細回饋意見。就像前面提過的，在構成段落的要素中，最重要的就是主題句。主題句必須概括段落的核心概念，也要夠有趣而能吸引讀者繼續讀下去。目前學生所寫的段落中，第一句（The trip to Barcelona totally changed my view about architecture）是段落的主題句。ChatGPT 會如何評價這個主題句呢？輸入提示詞如下。

Prompt

Give me some feedback on my topic sentence, which is the first sentence of the paragraph below.

對於我的主題句，也就是以下段落的第一句，給我一些回饋意見。

Your topic sentence, "The trip to Barcelona totally changed my view about architecture", effectively sets the stage for the rest of your paragraph and clearly conveys the main idea. It provides a preview of what the reader can expect to learn about in the following sentences. However, it might be even more effective if it was more specific and focused on a particular aspect of architecture that you will be discussing. For example, you could rephrase it as "My visit to Barcelona's unique and vibrant architecture, particularly the work of Gaudi, opened my eyes to the beauty and creativity of non-traditional building designs." This would make it clearer to the reader what aspect of architecture you will be discussing and make your topic sentence more engaging. Overall, though, your topic sentence does a good job of introducing your paragraph's main idea.

你的主題句「巴塞隆納之行徹底改變了我對建築的看法」有效地為段落的其餘部分做了鋪墊，並清晰地傳達了主旨。它預示了讀者可以預期在接下來的句子會了解到的內容。不過，如果更加具體，並且著重於你將要討論的建築的某個方面，效果可能會更好。例如，可以改寫為「我造訪巴塞隆納獨特而充滿活力的建築，尤其是高第的作品，讓我大開眼界，領略到非傳統建築設計的美感與創造力」。這樣會讓讀者更清楚知道你要討論的是建築的哪一方面，也會使你的主題句更有吸引力。但整體而言，你的主題句把段落的主旨介紹得很好。

ChatGPT 對於學生所寫的主題句給了很不錯的評價，並且給予回饋意見，建議聚焦於主題較具體的層面。此外，也提議把主題句寫成「My visit to Barcelona's unique and vibrant architecture, particularly the work of Gaudi, opened my eyes to the beauty and creativity of non-traditional building designs.」。

最後的結論句又如何呢？學生所寫的最後一個句子（It was so shocking and enjoyable experience that for a long time after I came back to Korea, I wanted to go back there just for the park Guell），顯示段落的結論，我們也請 ChatGPT 提供對於這個句子的回饋意見。

Prompt

Give me some feedback on my concluding sentence, which is the last sentence of the paragraph below.

對於我的結論句，也就是以下段落的最後一句，給我一些回饋意見。

Your concluding sentence effectively summarizes the main point of the paragraph and effectively communicates your newfound appreciation for architecture as a result of your trip to Barcelona. It conveys your desire to revisit the city and specifically mentions the Park Guell as a highlight of your trip. However, you could consider rephrasing the sentence to make it more concise and impactful, such as: "My trip to Barcelona, particularly the stunning architecture of Gaudi's Park Guell, left me with a newfound appreciation for the beauty of organic design, and a strong desire to return to the city."

你的結論句有效地概括了本段的要點，並有效地表達了你在巴塞隆納之行後對建築的新認識。它傳達了你重遊這座城市的願望，並特別提到奎爾公園是你此行的亮點。不過，你可以考慮重新措辭，使句子更簡潔、更有感染力，例如：「我的巴塞隆納之行，特別是造訪高第的奎爾公園令人驚嘆的建築，讓我對有機設計之美有了新的認識，並產生了重返這座城市的強烈願望。」

跟原本的句子比起來，ChatGPT 建議的結論句（My trip to Barcelona, particularly the stunning architecture of Gaudi's Park Guell, left me with a newfound appreciation for the beauty of organic design, and a strong desire to return to the city）做了更令人印象深刻的收尾，並且簡潔地總結了整體內容。

噢，我們還漏了一件事：這個段落沒有標題。我們請 ChatGPT 下適當的標題。

Please recommend three appropriate titles for the paragraph below.

請為下面的段落推薦三個適當的標題。

1. A Trip to Remember: How Barcelona's Architecture Changed Me

2. The Magic of Gaudi's Park Guell and Its Impact on My Perspective

3. Barcelona's Architectural Treasures: A Journey of Enlightenment

1. 難忘之旅：巴塞隆納的建築如何改變了我
2. 高第的奎爾公園的魔力，以及它對我觀點的影響
3. 巴塞隆納的建築瑰寶：啟蒙之旅

　　每次輸入提示詞時，結果都可能改變，因此可以輸入幾次相同的提示詞，選出其中最好的生成結果，也是不錯的方法。

　　接下來看看第二個段落寫作的例子。這次要寫描述段落（Descriptive Paragraph）。前面由學生所寫的記敘段落（Narrative Paragraph）是講述自己的經驗或事件，而描述段落則是仔細且生動地描繪一個對象或經驗。這次的題目是用一個段落描述自己最喜歡的地方。

題目2　Write a descriptive paragraph about your favorite place.
　　　　寫一個關於你最喜歡的地方的描述段落。

下面是學生在英文寫作課所寫的描述段落。

The Beautiful Library

My favorite place in my school, Seoul science high school, is the library. Recently, the library got repaired for several months and transformed into a beautiful. The library has lots of books and lots of seats to study of read books comfortably. Also, it has many fluffy seats to read books in a comfier environment. Focusing on the design, the library has a very modern and neat design. Its walls are covered with white color and the seats and the shelves are colored black. This color harmony makes a neat atmosphere. Also, there are some wooden pillars and many plants that promotes natural feelings for people. These designs make me visit the library more often. In conclusion, the library is one of the most beautiful places in the school because of its designs.

美麗的圖書館

我在我的學校——首爾科學高中——最喜歡的地方是圖書館。最近，圖書館經過幾個月的維修，變成一個美麗的。圖書館有很多書，還有很多座位，可以舒適地學習或看書。此外，這裡還有很多鬆軟的座位，可以在更舒服的環境中閱讀書籍。聚焦於設計，圖書館有非常現代而整潔的設計。牆壁以白色覆蓋，座位和書架是黑色的。這種色彩的調和營造出一種整潔的氛圍。此外，這裡還有一些木柱與許多植物，為人們增進自然的感覺。這些設計讓我更常去圖書館。總之，圖書館因為它的設計而是學校最美的地方之一。

寫出上面這段文章的學生，希望發揮描述性寫作的特性，所以用下面的提示詞來修改他的作文。

> **Prompt**
>
> 👤 Make this essay more natural using abundant expressions and emphasizing the beauty of the library. The title of the essay is 'The beautiful library'.
>
> 請使用豐富的表達方式，並強調圖書館的美麗，使這段文章更加自然。作文標題是「美麗的圖書館」。

⑤ Without a doubt, the library at Seoul Science High School is a true gem, and my personal favorite spot on campus. Recently, the library underwent a magnificent transformation that left it looking absolutely stunning. With an abundance of books and comfortable seating, this space is perfect for both reading and studying. What's more, the library features an array of plush chairs, offering the ultimate cozy reading experience. However, it's the library's design that truly sets it apart. Boasting a modern, sleek aesthetics, the library's walls are adorned with a pristine, pure white hue, while the seats and shelves are a sophisticated, deep black. This harmonious contrast creates an ambiance that is both refined and immaculate. Moreover, the presence of wooden pillars and greenery throughout the space invites a sense of natural tranquility, helping students to feel calm and focused. Truly, the library's striking design has become a personal source of inspiration for me, and I find myself drawn to the space time and time again. In conclusion, the library at Seoul Science High School is unequivocally one of the most beautiful places on campus, a true feast for the eyes and the soul.

毫無疑問，首爾科學高中的圖書館是真正的寶石（寶藏），也是我個人在校園裡最喜歡的地方。最近，圖書館經歷了一次華麗的蛻變，使它看起來極為令人驚嘆。這裡藏書豐富，座位舒適，是閱讀與學習的理想場所。此外，圖書館還有許多絨布椅子，提供極致的舒適閱讀體驗。不過，圖書館的設計才是真正與眾不同之處。圖書館的牆壁以純淨的白色為主色調，座椅和書架則是精緻的深黑色，呈現出現代、俐落的美學。這種和諧的對比營造出一種精緻又無瑕的氛圍。此外，貫穿整個空間的木柱與綠色植物帶來一種自然寧靜感，幫助學生們感到平靜且專注。的確，圖書館引人注目的設計已成為我個人靈感的源泉，我發現自己一次又一次地被這個空間所吸引。總之，首爾科學高中的圖書館無疑是校園裡最美麗的地方之一，是一場真正的視覺與心靈盛宴。

　　雖然 ChatGPT 把文章改得很美，但多了 true gem（真正的寶石）、magnificent transformation（華麗的蛻變）、ultimate cozy（極致舒適的）、a true feast for the eyes and the soul（真正的視覺與心靈盛宴）等描述，有些偏離了原本的表達方式。大概是因為給 ChatGPT 的提示詞中包含了

「abundant expressions」（豐富的表達方式），才產生了這種結果。我們改用下面的提示詞，讓它呈現出比較平淡，但文法上更自然、更接近描述性的寫作。以下提示詞賦予 ChatGPT 英語教師的角色，讓它提供改善文法與表達方式的回饋意見，並且展示稍微改善過的文章。這和記敘段落使用過的提示詞類似，不同之處在於要求提出改善版本的部分。

Prompt

Now you will become an English teacher and help me to improve the quality of my grammar and mainly the improve my adjectives.

me: <text>

you: <analyze the text and give recommendations and suggest an edited version>

現在，你將成為一名英語教師，幫我改善我的文法品質，主要是改善我的形容詞。

我：〈文本〉

你：〈分析文本並給出建議，以及提出編輯過的版本〉

Great job on your writing! Here are some suggestions to improve your grammar and adjectives:

-Instead of saying "transformed into a beautiful," try using more descriptive adjectives to paint a clearer picture for the reader. For example, you could say "transformed into a stunning, state-of-the-art facility."

-When describing the seats in the library, try to use more descriptive adjectives. For example, instead of "lots of seats," you could say "an abundance of comfortable, cushioned chairs and tables."

-Instead of using "comfier," you could say "more comfortable."

-Instead of saying "neat design," try using more specific adjectives like "sleek" or "minimalistic."

-Instead of using "promotes natural feelings," try using "creates a natural ambiance."

Here's an edited version of your text incorporating these suggestions:

My favorite place in my school, Seoul Science High School, is the library. Recently, the library underwent several months of repairs and transformed into a stunning, state-of-the-art facility. The library boasts an abundance of comfortable, cushioned chairs and tables to allow for a comfortable reading and studying environment. Additionally, the library features many sleek and modern fluffy seats, which add to the overall ambiance. The walls are painted white, creating a clean and minimalistic atmosphere, while the chairs and shelves are colored black, adding a touch of sophistication. The wooden pillars and beautiful foliage create a natural ambiance that makes me visit the library more often. In conclusion, the library is one of the most beautiful places in the school because of its sleek and modern design and its natural ambiance.

你的寫作很棒！以下是一些改進文法與形容詞的建議：

—不要說「變成一個美麗的」，而是嘗試使用描述性更強的形容詞，為讀者描繪出更清晰的畫面。例如，可以說「變成一座令人驚嘆的先進設施」。

－在描述圖書館的座位時，嘗試使用描述性更強的形容詞。例如，可以說「大量舒適的軟墊椅子與桌子」，而不是「很多座位」。

　　－用「更舒適」代替「更舒服」。

　　－不要說「整潔的設計」，可以嘗試使用「俐落」或「極簡」等更具體的形容詞。

　　－用「創造自然的氛圍」代替「促進自然的感覺」。

　　以下是你的文字納入以上建議編輯後的版本：

　　我在我的學校──首爾科學高中──最喜歡的地方是圖書館。最近，圖書館經過幾個月的維修，變成一座令人驚嘆的先進設施。圖書館擁有大量舒適的軟墊椅子與桌子，提供舒適的閱讀與學習環境。此外，圖書館還設有許多俐落而現代的絨布座綺，為整體氛圍增色。牆壁漆成白色，創造出乾淨極簡的氛圍，而椅子和書架則是黑色的，增添了一絲精緻感。木柱與美麗的樹葉創造出自然的氛圍，讓我更常去圖書館。總之，圖書館是學校最美的地方之一，因為它既有俐落而現代的設計，又有自然的氛圍。

和第一個修改版本比起來，第二個修改版本的文法與表達方式比較自然，也比較能呈現出原版的意圖與表達口吻。如同以上例子所顯示的，隨著提示詞的不同，ChatGPT 可能生成非常不同的結果。就連相同的提示，每次呈現的結果也可能稍有不同。重點在於，必須能夠判斷經過 ChatGPT 的回饋而修改的文章是否符合自己的意圖。不管詞藻再怎麼華麗，如果修改的版本添加了不符合原文意圖的內容，或者改變了文章整體的方向，那還不如不要改。如何接受 ChatGPT 的回饋意見，決定權在於寫作者本人。

段落寫作時使用的提示詞整理

這部分的最後，整理了學生們在英文寫作課請 ChatGPT 針對段落寫作給予回饋意見時所使用的提示詞。這些提示詞的要求，包括改成文法正確的文章、使文章更流暢、使描述性更強、增加連接詞而使句子之間連結更緊密（Connected）等等。希望各位讀者也用題目 1、2 的主題，先自己寫一個段落，然後再輸入以下各種提示詞，看看各種提示詞會產生什麼結果，找出什麼提示詞會讓你的文章產生最自然、最美好的變化。在追蹤這些變化之後，最終熟悉並練習，是最重要的。

學生在段落寫作時使用的提示詞整理

▶ Make the paragraph below more natural and polished, while maintaining the overall structure.

使以下段落更自然且精鍊，同時維持整體結構。

▶ Edit the following paragraph to make it more natural and fix grammar errors. The title of the paragraph is 'A lesson from the wound'. Then, also tell me the parts you fixed.

編輯以下段落，使它更自然，並且修正文法錯誤。段落的標題是「創傷帶來的教訓」。然後，也告訴我你修正的部分。

▶ Make my paragraph more fluent.

使我的段落更流暢。

▶ Correct the grammar in the paragraph below.

修正以下段落的文法。

▶ Can you make the expressions stronger?

你可以讓表達方式更強烈嗎？

▶ Can you make a proper title for this writing?

你可以給這段作文取個適合的標題嗎？

▶ Make the paragraph visually clear.

使這個段落的畫面變得清晰。

▶ Correct grammatical errors or change words to more vivid and complicated ones.

修正文法錯誤，或者將單字換成更生動、更複雜的。

▶ Make the paragraph below more effective while unchanging the story.

使以下段落更有效果，同時不改變故事。

▶ Find grammatical errors in the following paragraph and improve my paragraph.

找出以下段落的文法錯誤，並且改善我的段落。

▶ Can you make the sentences more connected for the paragraph below?

對於以下的段落，你可以讓句子連結更緊密嗎？

▶ Can you make my descriptive paragraph more interesting, connecting the sentences more naturally?

你可以讓我的描述段落更有趣，同時更自然地將句子連結起來嗎？

▶ Please refine this following paragraph.

請對以下段落進行潤色。

▶ How can I improve this paragraph?

我可以怎樣改善這個段落？

▶ I intended the sentences to be short. Can you make the sentences shorter?

我希望句子是簡短的。你可以把句子變短嗎？

▶ Rewrite this paragraph with more descriptive words.

用比較多的描述性詞語重寫這個段落。

▶ Describe more about board game cafes based on this paragraph.

根據這個段落，對桌遊咖啡店做更多描述。

- The paragraph below is a descriptive paragraph about my house. Please improve it for better understanding.

  以下段落是關於我家房子的描述段落。請改善它，使它更易懂。

- Make it more descriptive and make it into one paragraph.

  使它更有描述性，並且把它變成一個段落。

- Please convert its expressions and refine its flow.

  請改變它的表達方式，並且改善它的流暢性。

- Make my paragraph more descriptive and neat.

  使我的段落更有描述性而且簡潔。

- Paraphrase my sentences so they are more concise.

  改寫我的句子，使它們更簡潔。

- Adjust my vocabulary usage so the paragraph is more natural.

  調整我的詞彙使用，使段落更自然。

- Combine some sentences that could be shortened.

  合併一些可以被縮短的句子。

- Change a few words in this paragraph and make it more fancy.

  改變這個段落的一些單字，使它花俏些。

- Make the paragraph more fluent.

  使這個段落更流暢。

- Please provide the text you would like me to edit and transform it into a descriptive paragraph.

  請給我你希望我編輯的文字，並且把它轉變成描述段落。

用 ChatGPT 輔助短文寫作

　　前面我們對於段落寫作進行了探討。簡單來說，段落是處理同一主題的一些句子的結合體，主題句則是呈現段落核心概念最重要的句子。接下來，就要正式探討短文寫作了。

從段落到短文

　　段落和短文的差異是什麼？這裡我們也先問 ChatGPT 看看。

Prompt

　　　段落和短文的差異是什麼？

⑥ 段落是由多個句子構成，聚焦於一個想法或主題的文章寫作單位。一般而言，段落的第一個句子是介紹段落主要想法的主題句，之後則加上提供細節與例子的支持句。另一方面，短文則是指由幾個段落構成、比較長的寫作型態。一般而言，短文會在前言部分（Introduction）寫出短文主要的主題或主旨陳述句（Thesis Statement），之後則接幾個段落，用證據與分析將主旨陳述句推展開來。最後，短文通常都有結論部分（Conclusion），總結主要重點並以新的方式重新表達主旨陳述句。也就是說，段落是短文的構成要素之一，而多個段落則構成短文。段落與短文都聚焦於一個想法，但短文涵蓋範圍較廣，並且提供詳細的探討。

我們可以從以上內容得知段落與短文的差異。簡單來說，短文是由多個段落構成的寫作型態，目的是讓人深入理解一個主題或論題。短文通常由前言（Introduction）、正文（Body）、結論（Conclusion）構成。前言介紹主題，正文從各方面探討論題，而結論總結整體的討論，並且對主題提出新的視角。那麼，要怎樣將段落擴展成短文呢？請看下表。

Paragraph		Essay
Topic Sentence ➡	Introduction	Thesis Statement
Supporting Sentence 1 ➡		Supporting Paragraph 1
Supporting Sentence 2 ➡	Body	Supporting Paragraph 2
Supporting Sentence 3 ➡		Supporting Paragraph 3
Concluding Sentence ➡	Conclusion	Conclusion

將段落擴展成短文

　　段落中最重要的句子，也就是主題句，會變成短文裡前言段落的主旨陳述句。也就是說，主旨陳述句就像主題句一樣，必須表明寫這篇文章的理由、目的與核心概念。而段落中包含細節資訊的每個句子，都會各自發展成為一個段落。最後，段落的結論句則會變成短文的結論段落。下表進一步詳細說明短文的結構。

Introduction （前言：1 段）		Hook	文章的第一句，吸引讀者注意的句子（例如以問題、格言、名言、故事等開始）
		Background Information	引言（Hook）與主旨陳述句（Thesis Statement）之間的連結。說明短文討論內容的背景。
		Thesis Statement	通常是前言段落的最後一句，表示短文的核心主張。
Body （正文： 3-4 段）	Supporting Paragraph 2, 3, 4 每段的結構	Topic Sentence	呈現該段落要探討的核心
		Supporting Details	提出支持主題句的具體內容
		Transition Sentence	幫助從目前段落轉移到下個段落的句子
Conclusion （結論：1 段）		Restated Thesis	總結正文部分探討的內容，並強調主張。重新呈現主旨陳述句
		Suggestion, opinion, or prediction	提出與主題相關的啟示

短文的結構

　　以下用 ChatGPT 生成有五個段落的短文，從具體的例子探討文章的整體結構。

Write a 5-paragraph narrative essay about 'A Life-Changing Trip Abroad'

寫一篇關於「一次改變人生的海外旅行」的五段記敘短文

(Hook) Traveling abroad can be a life-changing experience for many people. (Background Information) It is a chance to explore new cultures, meet new people, and learn new things. My life-changing trip abroad happened a few years ago when I decided to take a gap year after finishing high school. I had always wanted to travel and experience different cultures, but I had never had the opportunity to do so until then. (Thesis Statement) I chose to travel to Southeast Asia, and it turned out to be the best decision I ever made.

(Topic Sentence 1) As soon as I arrived in Southeast Asia, I was struck by the beauty of the landscape, the warmth of the people, and the rich culture. (Supporting Details) I traveled through Thailand, Vietnam, Cambodia, and Laos, and each country had its unique charm. I was able to visit temples, try new foods, and learn about the history and customs of each country. One of my most memorable experiences was visiting Angkor Wat in Cambodia, an ancient temple complex that took my breath away.

(Topic Sentence 2) However, my trip was not all sunshine and rainbows. I had to face many challenges, including language barriers and cultural differences. (Supporting Details) It was challenging to communicate with locals in some areas, and I had to rely on hand gestures and basic phrases to get by. Moreover, some cultural practices were very different from what I was used to, and it took me a while to adapt. But despite these challenges, I found that I was growing as a person, becoming more adaptable and open-minded.

(Topic Sentence 3) The most significant impact of my trip abroad was the people I met along the way. (Supporting Details) I made friends with locals and fellow travelers who came from all over the world. We shared stories and experiences, and I learned so much from them. One of my closest friends on the trip was a local tour guide who showed me around his city and introduced me to his family. It was incredible to see how different their lives were from mine, but also how similar we were in many ways.

(Restated Thesis) In conclusion, my trip abroad was truly life-changing. I came back home with a broader perspective on the world, a deeper understanding of different cultures, and a newfound appreciation for the small things in life. I also gained valuable skills such as adaptability, independence, and communication. (Suggestion) I encourage anyone who has the opportunity to travel abroad to do so, as it can be a transformative experience that will stay with you for a lifetime.

對許多人來說，出國旅行可能會是改變人生的經歷。這是探索新文化、結識新朋友、學習新事物的機會。改變我一生的國外旅行發生在幾年前，當時我決定在高中畢業後空出一年。當時我一直想去旅行，體驗不同的文化，但在那之前我從來沒有這樣的機會。我選擇了去東南亞旅行，結果證明這是我做過最好的決定。

一到東南亞，我就被風景之美、人民的熱情和豐富的文化所感動。我遊歷了泰國、越南、柬埔寨和寮國，每個國家都有獨特的魅力。我得以參觀寺廟、品嚐新的食物、了解每個國家的歷史與習俗。我最難忘的經歷之一是參觀柬埔寨的吳哥窟，這座古老的寺廟建築群讓我嘆為觀止。

然而，我的旅行並不全是陽光和彩虹。我必須面對許多挑戰，包括語言障礙與文化差異。在某些地區，與當地人溝通是一項挑戰，我不得不依靠手勢和基本片語來應對。此外，有些文化習俗和我習慣的很不一樣，花了我一段時間適應。不過，儘管有這些挑戰，我發現自己在成長，變得更有適應力，思想也更開放。

出國旅行對我影響最大的是一路上遇到的人。我和當地人以及來自世界各地的旅人成為了朋友。我們分享故事與經歷，而我從他們身上學到了很多。我在旅途中最親密的朋友之一是當地的導遊，他帶我參觀了他的城市，並且向我介紹了他的家人。看到他們的生活與我的生活如此不同，但我們在很多方面又如此相似，真是不可思議。

總之，我的海外旅行確實改變了我的人生。回國後，我對世界有了更開闊的觀點，對不同文化有了更深入的了解，對生活中的小事也有了新的認識。我也獲得了寶貴的技能，例如適應能力、獨立性和溝通能力。我鼓勵任何有機會出國旅行的人都去做，因為這可能是會改變你一生的經歷。

首先簡單地概述每個段落，掌握短文的核心內容。

👤 Summarize the main idea of each paragraph briefly.

簡短概述每一段的主旨。

⑤ Sure, here's a brief summary of the main idea of each paragraph in the essay:

- Paragraph 1: The opening paragraph establishes the central theme of the essay, which is the transformative power of travel, and introduces the topic of a life-changing trip abroad.

- Paragraph 2: The second paragraph describes the author's initial impressions upon arriving in Southeast Asia, including the beauty of the landscape, the warmth of the people, and the rich culture.

- Paragraph 3: The third paragraph highlights the challenges that the author faced during their trip, including language barriers and cultural differences.

- Paragraph 4: The fourth paragraph discusses the most significant impact of the author's trip abroad, which was the people they met along the way, including locals and fellow travelers.

- Paragraph 5: The final paragraph contains the thesis statement of the essay and provides a conclusion to the author's experience, emphasizing how their trip was truly life-changing and encouraging others to travel abroad.

當然，以下是這篇短文每一段的主旨概述：

－第一段：開頭的段落確立了短文的中心主題，也就是旅行的改變力量，並引出了改變人生的國外旅行這個話題。

－第二段：第二段描述了作者抵達東南亞的最初印象，包括風景之美、人民的熱情與豐富的文化。

－第三段：第三段重點介紹了作者在旅途中面臨的挑戰，包括語言障礙與文化差異。

－第四段：第四段討論了作者海外之行的最大影響，也就是沿途遇到的人，包括當地人與同行的旅人。

－第五段：最後一段包含這篇短文的主旨陳述，並且總結作者的經歷，強調這次旅行如何真正改變了人生，並鼓勵其他人出國旅行。

現在我們一一檢視文章的成分。第一段（Paragraph 1）是前言。如同前面介紹過的，前言由吸引讀者注意的引言（Hook）、短文的背景說明（Background Information），以及呈現文章最核心內容的主旨陳述句（Thesis Statement）構成。為了更仔細分析這篇短文的前言部分，我們提出下面的問題。

Prompt

Where is the hook?

引言在哪裡？

The hook in the essay is the first sentence that catches the reader's attention and makes them want to keep reading. In this essay, the hook is the opening sentence: "Traveling abroad can be a life-changing experience for many people." This sentence immediately sets the tone for the essay and establishes the central theme of the essay - the transformative power of travel. It also creates curiosity in the reader's mind and encourages them to read further to find out more about the author's personal experience of a life-changing trip abroad.

短文中的引言是吸引讀者的注意力、讓他們想要繼續閱讀的第一句話。在這篇短文中,引言是開頭的句子:「對許多人來說,出國旅行可能會是改變人生的經歷。」這句話立即為文章定下了基調,並確立了文章的中心主題——旅行的改變力量。這句話還會在讀者心中產生好奇心,鼓勵他們進一步閱讀,了解作者關於改變人生的海外之旅的個人經歷。

👤 Where is the thesis statement in the first paragraph?

第一段的主旨陳述句在哪裡？

🌀 Although a thesis statement can be placed in different parts of an essay, it is generally found in the introduction or the conclusion. In this essay, the thesis statement is not explicitly stated in the first paragraph. However, the first paragraph sets the context for the essay by introducing the topic of a life-changing trip abroad and providing a brief overview of the author's experience. The final sentence of the first paragraph, "It turned out to be the best decision I ever made," hints at the main idea of the essay but does not clearly state the thesis. Instead, the thesis statement is presented in the conclusion of the essay.

雖然主旨陳述句可以放在文章的不同部分，但通常都在前言或結論之中。在這篇短文裡，第一段並沒有明確做出主旨陳述。不過，第一段透過介紹改變人生的國外旅行這個主題，以及簡要概述作者的經歷，為這篇短文設定了背景。第一段的最後一句「結果證明這是我做過最好的決定」暗示了這篇短文的主旨，但沒有清楚表明主旨。相反地，主旨陳述是在這篇短文的結論中提出。

ChatGPT 掌握到前言的最後一句（I chose to travel to Southeast Asia, and it turned out to be the best decision I ever made）隱含了文章核心的主旨陳述，但不是明確表現出來。而這個句子在結論部分重新陳述了一遍。

接下來讓我們看看正文部分。構成正文的每一段，都由主題句與支持主題句的內容組成。我們問問 ChatGPT，這篇短文每一段的主題句在哪裡？

Prompt

👤 List the topic sentences in the paragraphs 2, 3, and 4.

列出第二、三、四段的主題句。

Sure, here are the topic sentences for each of the three body paragraphs in the essay:

- Paragraph 2: "As soon as I arrived in Southeast Asia, I was struck by the beauty of the landscape, the warmth of the people, and the rich culture."

- Paragraph 3: "However, my trip was not all sunshine and rainbows. I had to face many challenges, including language barriers and cultural differences."

- Paragraph 4: "The most significant impact of my trip abroad was the people I met along the way."

當然，以下是這篇短文正文部分三個段落的主題句：

－第二段：「一到東南亞，我就被風景之美、人民的熱情和豐富的文化所感動。」

－第三段：「然而，我的旅行並不全是陽光和彩虹。我必須面對許多挑戰，包括語言障礙與文化差異。」

－第四段：「出國旅行對我影響最大的是一路上遇到的人。」

ChatGPT 列出每段的第一句作為主題句。而在主題句後面的句子，全部都是支持主題句的內容。

最後來看看結論部分。結論段落會重述正文部分討論的要點，並且指出與主題相關的意義或啟示。尤其藉由重提前言部分的主旨陳述，結論段落能讓人想起短文中最重要的內容。

Prompt

Where is the thesis statement in the last paragraph?

最後一段的主旨陳述在哪裡？

The thesis statement in this essay is located in the last paragraph of the essay, which begins with the sentence "In conclusion, my trip abroad was truly life-changing." This sentence summarizes the main idea of the essay and restates the author's thesis, which is that traveling abroad can be a life-changing experience. The following sentences in the concluding paragraph further explain the impact of the trip on the author's personal growth and development, emphasizing how the trip broadened their perspective, deepened their understanding of different cultures, and increased their appreciation for the small things in life. The concluding paragraph ends with a call to action, encouraging readers to take the opportunity to travel abroad themselves and experience the transformative power of travel.

　　這篇短文的主旨陳述在文章的最後一段,這一段以「總之,我的海外旅行確實改變了我的人生」這句話開頭。這句話概括了文章的主旨,並且重申了作者的主要論點,也就是出國旅行可能會是改變人生的經驗。結論段落接下來的句子,進一步解釋了這次旅行對作者個人成長與發展的影響,強調這次旅行如何開拓作者的視野、加深對不同文化的理解,並且提高了對生活中小事的認識。結論段落的結尾呼籲讀者採取行動,鼓勵他們把握機會出國旅行,體驗旅行改變的力量。

　　我們分析了 ChatGPT 生成的記敘短文〈A Life-Changing Trip Abroad〉,並且仔細探討了文章的結構。熟悉文章的基本構造,是寫出有效的文章之前必要的工作。接下來,我們要探討短文的類型。

短文的類型

　　世界上有許許多多的文章，文章的種類也非常多元。不過，我們英文寫作課的目標是撰寫短文，並且會從各種短文中選出最具代表性的類型來討論。因為在課堂上要討論哪種短文類型也很重要，所以用下面的提示詞請ChatGPT 提供建議。

Prompt

🙎 Show me four popular essay genres and list some example topics.

告訴我四種常見的短文類型，並且列出一些主題的例子。

🌀　Certainly! Here are four popular essay genres with some examples of topics:

　　- Narrative Essay: This genre involves telling a story or describing a personal experience.

"The Day I Got Lost in the Wilderness"

"My First Day of High School"

"A Life-Changing Trip Abroad"

- Descriptive Essay: This genre involves using sensory details to paint a vivid picture of a person, place, or thing.

"The Serenity of a Beach Sunset"

"The Bustling City Streets of New York"

"The Sweet Aroma of Freshly Baked Cookies"

- Expository Essay: This genre involves explaining or describing a concept or idea in detail.

"The Process of Photosynthesis"

"The History of the Internet"

"The Effects of Social Media on Mental Health"

- Argumentative Essay (Persuasive Essay): This genre involves presenting an argument and attempting to persuade the reader to agree with your point of view.

"Why Recycling Should be Mandatory"

"The Benefits of Exercise for Mental Health"

"The Importance of Learning a Second Language"

當然！以下是四種常見的短文類型，以及一些主題的例子：

－記敘文：這種類型講述一個故事或描述一段個人經歷。

「我在荒野迷路的那一天」

「我上高中的第一天」

「一次改變人生的海外旅行」

－描述文：這種類型用感官細節來描繪人物、地點或事物的生動畫面。

「海灘夕陽的寧靜」

「紐約熙熙攘攘的街道」

「剛烤好的餅乾甜香」

－說明文：這種類型詳細解釋或描述一個概念或想法。

「光合作用的過程」

「網際網路的歷史」

「社交媒體對心理健康的影響」

－論說文（說服性文章）：這種類型提出論點並試圖說服讀者同意你的觀點。

「為什麼應該強制資源回收」

「運動對心理健康的益處」

「學習第二語言的重要性」

ChatGPT 列出記敘文、描述文、說明文、論說文這幾種最重要的文章類型。我們也將在課堂中探討這四種類型的短文。接下來，就讓我們逐一了解一下。

第一種是記敘文，內容是個人的故事，依照時間順序記敘事件的開始－中途－結局。從個人經驗到虛構的故事等各種主題，都可以寫成記敘文。記敘文的結論通常會寫到經由事件而學到的事、事件為作者的人生帶來的教訓或啟示等。

第二種是描述文。從名稱可以知道，這種文章是詳細描述一個對象或經驗。這種類型的文章會用感官上的細節與生動的語言，將主題栩栩如生地表現出來。在前言與結論部分，通常會表明描述某個對象的理由。

第三種是說明文，內容是針對主題做出平衡的分析，並透過證據與例子說明主題。其中代表性的類型有比較對照文（Compare and Contrast Essay）與因果關係文（Cause and Effect Essay）。

最後一種是論說文，也稱為說服性文章（Persuasive Essay），目的是說服讀者接受作者的觀點或採取特定行動。作者會用適當的證據表達自己明確的主張，最後用有力的結論讓讀者留下深刻的印象。

以上介紹了四種代表性的短文類型。記敘文與描述文在敘事與描寫方面有許多相似處，因為它們都經常在展開敘事的同時，自然地加入描述性的內容。而說明文與論說文也有許多共通點，因為在對特定主題提出主張之前，往往需要對主題進行有條理的說明。所以，類型之間的界線實際上經常是曖昧模糊的。不過，還是要知道文章有記敘、描述、說明、論說等不同的目的。

現在我們已經知道短文的類型，接著就來看看實際撰寫短文時會經歷什麼過程。

短文寫作的六個階段

好的文章不會像變魔術般一下子就寫好。要寫出好文章，必須經歷一些寫作的階段。我們先問 ChatGPT 下面的問題。

Prompt

請告訴我撰寫短文的六個階段。

撰寫短文的六個階段如下。

1. 選定主題

撰寫短文之前要先選定主題。主題可以是自己感興趣的領域或經驗、事件、現象等各種事物。

2. 思考構想

選定主題後，就要收集構想。透過資料調查收集相關資訊，綜合後產生新的構想。

3. 撰寫大綱

將構想具體化並整理之後，必須撰寫大綱。大綱訂定文章的結構，其中必須包含前言、正文、結論等內容。

4. 撰寫草稿

　　這個階段以大綱為基礎來撰寫文章。這時候，應該著重於內容與結構。在這個階段，即使寫得不完美也沒關係，重要的是加入內容。

5. 修正與編輯

　　撰寫草稿後，要取得回饋意見並進行修正。這時候，應該確認文章的前後承接是否自然流暢、句子是否明確而不會太長、拼字與文法是否正確等等。

6. 撰寫最終版本

　　修正完成後，短文就完成了。這時候，應該再次檢查錯字、文法、邏輯、表達方式等等，並思考是否有更好的表達方法。預留充分的時間，確保能遵守交稿期限，最後在檢查後交稿。

選定主題 ・探索主題	思考構想 ・產生構想 ・選定構想	撰寫大綱 ・組織構想	撰寫草稿 ・產生文本 ・1st draft	修正與編輯 ・ChatGPT / peer feedback ・Self-editing ・2nd / 3nd draft	撰寫 最終版本 ・潤稿 ・Final draft

短文寫作的六個階段

ChatGPT 詳細介紹了寫出好文章的六個階段。第一到第三階段是在寫作前為了撰寫草稿而描繪文章藍圖的階段。在寫作前的階段，會收集撰寫文章所需的資訊，並且將構想組織起來。事實上，這個階段和實際寫文章的階段一樣重要。在實務中，許多學生在學習寫作初期常說「不知道該寫什麼」或「不知道該怎麼整理出要寫的內容」，表露在產出寫作內容方面遇到的困難。所以在寫文章之前，為寫作進行周密的準備真的很重要。而從第四階段開始，就是將寫作前階段構想的內容用文字實際寫出來的過程。之後透過第五、六階段，學生能使文章的意義漸漸變得清晰。「4. 撰寫草稿」的階段會產生初稿（1st draft），「5. 修正與編輯」階段會產生二稿（2nd draft）[11]，而最後「6. 撰寫最終版本」階段會產生最終版本（final draft）。

接下來，要進一步詳細探討前面提過的四種短文類型（Narrative, Descriptive, Expository, Argumentative Essay）寫作過程的各個階段。為了實際觀察從構想階段到文章完成階段的過程，我們將跟隨四名英文寫作課學生的寫作歷程。另外，我們也將觀察學生在寫作各階段如何應用 ChatGPT。

---

11 ChatGPT 或同儕提供回饋意見後，檢視自己的文章，如果還有額外的修正，也可以寫第三份草稿（3rd draft）、第四份草稿（4th draft）。

成品導向法 (Product-Oriented Writing Approach) vs.
過程導向法 (Process-Oriented Writing Approach)

寫作有兩種代表性的教學方式，分別是成品導向法與過程導向法。
成品導向法是指將指導的重點放在學生產出的文章，也就是寫作的
結果。相反地，過程導向法則是指教學著重於寫作者在過程中經歷
的階段，多過關注寫作的結果。因此，成品導向法強調要求學生模
仿範例段落或範例文章。過程導向法則是觀察熟練寫作者的寫作過
程，進而設定寫作時必須經歷的階段，然後讓學生在寫文章時依照
這樣的過程來寫。

歷史上，早期的寫作教學方式是成品導向法。但後來逐漸轉向過程
導向法，也出現了適度混合、應用成品導向法與過程導向法的寫作
方式。在本書中，比起寫作的成品，更重視產出成品的創意過程，
因此是以過程導向法為基礎。

各類型短文的寫作

記敘文（Narrative Essay）：敏奎的寫作

敏奎要把自己的故事寫成文章。我們分階段來看敏奎的寫作過程。

Step 1. 選定主題

記敘文是針對事件、經驗、狀況敘述個人故事的寫作形式，主要表達透過自己的經驗而得到的教訓、想法、情緒，主題範圍從日常經驗到特別的體驗等等，相當多元。敏奎還沒想到記敘文的主題，所以對 ChatGPT 提出下面的要求。

Prompt

👤 Recommend good topics for a narrative essay.

請推薦適合寫成記敘文的主題。

🌀 A good topic for a narrative essay is a personal experience that has taught you an important lesson or had a significant impact on your life. This could be an event that changed your perspective, a moment that challenged you, or a memory that shaped who you are today. Here are some ideas to get you started:

1. A time when you faced a fear or overcame a challenge

2. A moment that changed your perspective on life

3. An experience that taught you the importance of friendship or family

4. A memorable travel experience

5. An event that inspired you to pursue a particular career or passion

6. A lesson you learned from a mistake or failure

7. A childhood memory that has stayed with you

8. A relationship that impacted your life

9. A significant accomplishment that you achieved

10. A moment that taught you the value of perseverance or resilience

好的記敘文主題,是給你上了重要的一課,或對你的人生產生了重大影響的個人經歷。它可以是改變了你觀點的一件事,也可以是對你造成挑戰的一個時刻,或者是塑造了今天的你的一段回憶。以下是一些可以幫助你開始寫作的想法：

1. 你面臨恐懼或克服挑戰的時刻

2. 改變你人生觀的時刻

3. 讓你懂得友情或親情重要性的經歷

4. 一次難忘的旅行經歷

5. 激勵你追求特定職業或愛好的事件

6. 從錯誤或失敗中學到的教訓

7. 仍然記在你心中的童年回憶

8. 影響你人生的一段關係

9. 你達成的一項重大成就

10. 讓你懂得堅持不懈或心理韌性的價值的時刻

Step 2. 思考構想

敏奎瀏覽 ChatGPT 建議的這些主題，他注意到其中「一次難忘的旅行經歷」（4. A memorable travel experience）這一項。敏奎記得小時候曾經和家人一起去美國旅行，相對於出發前很高的期待，實際的美國之旅非常令人失望。他想著是不是可以把這個故事寫成短文。為了想出對於這個主題更具體的構想，敏奎在 ChatGPT 輸入了以下提示詞。

I have a childhood memory of traveling to the United States with my family and being very disappointed at the actual trip, in contrast to the great expectations I had before departure. I want to write about it in a narrative essay in chronological order, and I need you to brainstorm ideas for this essay.

在我童年的記憶中,我曾經和家人一起去美國旅行,但相對於我在出發之前很大的期待,實際上的旅行卻讓我非常失望。我想按時間順序把它寫成記敘文,而我需要你為這篇短文腦力激盪出一些構想。

Sure, here are some ideas for your narrative essay:

– Introduction:

- Begin with an anecdote or description of your expectations before the trip.
- Provide some background information about the trip, such as the reason for it, who went, and how old you were at the time.
- End with a thesis statement that expresses the

main point of the essay.

- Paragraph 1: Pre-trip excitement
  - Describe your anticipation and excitement leading up to the trip, including the planning and preparation that went into it.
  - Explain what you were looking forward to experiencing in the United States.
  - Include sensory details and emotions to help the reader understand your perspective.
- Paragraph 2: Travel and arrival
  - Describe the journey to the United States, including any airports, flights, or modes of transportation.
  - Explain how you felt during the journey and upon arrival in the United States.
  - Include any initial impressions you had of the country or culture.
- Paragraph 3: Reality sets in
  - Describe the moments when you realized that the trip was not going to meet your expectations.
  - Explain the specific reasons why you were disappointed, such as the weather, accommodations, or activities.

- Include any reactions or emotions you had in response to the disappointment.
  - Paragraph 4: Coping with disappointment
    - Describe how you coped with the disappointment, such as trying to find alternative activities or distracting yourself with something else.
    - Explain any positive experiences you had on the trip despite the disappointment, such as bonding with family members or discovering something unexpected.
    - Include any reflections you had about how to handle disappointment in the future.
  - Paragraph 5: Lessons learned
    - Summarize the lessons you learned from the experience, such as how to manage expectations, the importance of flexibility, or the value of perspective.
    - Explain how the experience has impacted you since then.
    - End with a concluding statement that ties together the main points of the essay and offers some final thoughts.

當然，以下是對於你的記敘文的一些構想：

– 前言：

- 以趣聞軼事或描述旅行前的期望開頭。

- 提供關於這次旅行的一些背景資訊，例如旅行的原因、誰去了、當時你多大。

- 最後用主旨陳述句來表達文章的要點。

– 第 1 段：旅行前的興奮

- 描述你在旅行前的期待與興奮，包括旅行前的計畫與準備。

- 說明你期待在美國經歷什麼。

- 包含感官細節與情緒，幫助讀者了解你的觀點。

– 第 2 段：旅行與抵達

- 描述前往美國的旅程，包括任何機場、航班或交通方式。

- 說明你在旅途中和抵達美國後的感受。

- 包含你對這個國家或文化最初的任何印象。

– 第 3 段：現實的到來

- 描述你意識到這次旅行無法滿足你的期望的時刻。

- 說明你感到失望的具體原因，例如天氣、住宿或活動。

- 包含你對失望的任何反應或情緒。

- 第 4 段：應對失望
  - 描述你如何應對失望，例如嘗試尋找替代的活動，或者用其他事情分散注意力。
  - 說明你在旅途中儘管失望，但仍然有過的任何正面經驗，例如與家人建立親密關係，或者意料之外的發現。
  - 包含你對於未來如何處理失望的反思。
- 第 5 段：學到的教訓
  - 總結你從這次經歷中學到的教訓，例如怎樣管控期待、保持彈性的重要性，或者觀點的價值。
  - 說明這次經驗往後對你的影響。
  - 用結合短文要點的結語收尾，並提出一些最後的想法。

Step 3. 撰寫大綱

敏奎在 Step 2 藉由 ChatGPT 的幫助，為「令人失望的旅行」這個短文主題生成了文章中將包含的一些構想。為了寫出實際的文章，在 Step 3 要將構想具體化，並且組織出文章必須具備的框架（大綱）。這裡也請 ChatGPT 幫忙，輸入的提示詞如下。

Prompt

I have a childhood memory of traveling to the United States with my family and being very disappointed at the actual trip, in contrast to the great expectations I had before departure. I want to write about it in a narrative essay in chronological order, and I need you to make a 5-paragraph narrative essay outline.

在我童年的記憶中,我曾經和家人一起去美國旅行,但相對於我在出發之前很大的期待,實際上的旅行卻讓我非常失望。我想按時間順序把它寫成記敘文,而我需要你寫出有五段內容的記敘文大綱。

Sure, I can help you with that! Here's a 5-paragraph narrative essay outline on your childhood memory of traveling to the United States:

I. Introduction

A. Hook: A brief description of your childhood memory of traveling to the United States and the disappointment you felt

B. Background information: Why you were excited to go to the United States

C. Thesis statement: Despite having great expectations for the trip, your actual experience in the United States was disappointing.

II. Pre-Departure Excitement
A. Description of your anticipation leading up to the trip
B. The preparations made for the trip
C. Your expectations of the United States based on what you had seen in the media

III. Arrival and Initial Impressions
A. Description of your first impressions of the United States
B. Contrast between your expectations and reality
C. The disappointment you felt during your first days in the United States

IV. Disappointing Experiences
A. Description of specific experiences that disappointed you
B. Examples of cultural differences that were difficult to adjust to

C. The impact of these experiences on your overall impression of the United States

V. Conclusion

A. Recap of the disappointment you felt during the trip

B. Reflection on how this experience has shaped your perspective on travel and expectations

C. Final thoughts on the importance of managing expectations when traveling to new places.

當然，我可以幫忙！以下是關於你童年時到美國旅行的回憶的五段記敘文大綱：

I. 前言

A. 引言：簡要描述你童年時到美國旅行的回憶，以及當時感受到的失望

B. 背景資訊：你為什麼對於去美國感到興奮

C. 主旨陳述句：儘管對這次旅行有很大的期待，但你在美國的實際經歷卻令人失望。

II. 出發前的興奮

A. 描述你對這次旅行的期待

B. 為旅行所做的準備

C. 你根據在媒體上看到的印象，而對美國產生的期望

III. 抵達與初步印象

A. 描述你對美國的第一印象

B. 你的期望與現實的對比

C. 在美國的前幾天感受到的失望

IV. 令人失望的經驗

A. 描述令你失望的具體經驗

B. 難以適應的文化差異實例

C. 這些經驗對你的美國整體印象的影響

V. 結論

A. 回顧你在旅行中感受到的失望

B. 反思這次經驗如何形塑了你對旅行與期望的觀點

C. 最後，對於去新地方旅行時管控期望的重要性分享想法。

Step 4. 撰寫草稿

終於完成大綱了。而在這個階段,要以完成的大綱為基礎,自己撰寫文章。這時候,確認文章整體結構,並且在這個結構的基礎上填入內容,比細部的表達方式和文法來得重要。此外,在這個階段,文章的獨創性非常重要。在我們的英文寫作課,這個階段特別強調禁止使用 ChatGPT 等 AI 工具,而要靠自己寫出草稿。尤其是記敘文,如果靠 ChatGPT 撰寫草稿的話,只會產生不包含自己的經驗、毫無特色的文章。以下是敏奎以前面完成的大綱為基礎,在課堂上自己寫出來的草稿。

My Trip to America

(1st draft)

To a young child like me, America was a dreamland full of opportunity and hope. That was why I eagerly looked forward to our family trip to the Eastern States. I expected my travel to be one of the most fantastic experiences in my entire life. However, what I found before long was my hope shattered through the rushing winds of reality, and a bitter wave of disappointment.

Before the flight, I was very delighted and joyfully waited the day of departure. The day eventually came in front of me. Full of anticipation, our family started the boarding procedures hours before the flight. After the check-in, we waited a long time, predicting about what will happen half the globe away. Finally, the time came, and we all boarded on the plane. It was my first experience on a flight for such a long time. My parents told me to sleep, but I could hardly close my eyes, watching the magnificent midair view, which lessened my sleeping time. Naturally I lost track of time, and when the plane arrived, I was exhausted. My family were also tired because of the huge time difference. Nevertheless, the guide came and the tour immediately started. We began our journey riding on the lengthy travel bus.

The summer sunshine was blazing and there were no shades on the bus. Most the clothes I prepared were short-sleeved, so I unintendedly took a sunbath until nightfall. The bus often stopped and we were told to enter some attractions. But under the sweltering heat, it was even difficult to open my eyes and see the buildings. I started to feel regret about planning the trip. I looked into my family, wondering if it is just me. My mom also seemed to be worn out as me. My dad and my brother were slightly better than us, but were not very different. As we headed to the restaurant for dinner, I was grateful that the daily schedule has finally ended. After dinner, we all quickly headed to the hotel and fell into a deep sleep.

Next morning, I still had the jet lag, but was in much better shape. Now my eyes started to catch sight of the scenery around myself. What I found was just a large town, having no much difference with Korea. I had expected something very special, which I cannot even imagine before the trip, but it turned out to be false. The only things new were some historical sites and natural heritages, but I was not that interested on them. What I wanted was a high-tech city similar to those on the movies.

The ten days in America passed quickly, mostly because I was sleeping on the bus. When I returned home, I was depressing that almost half of the summer vacation just disappeared without any memorable moments. After the failure, I started to dislike traveling abroad. It continued until three years after when my family scheduled a trip to Singapore.

我的美國之旅

（初稿）

　　對於像我這樣年幼的孩子，美國曾經是充滿機會與希望的夢幻國度。正因如此，我（當時）熱切地盼望我們去美國東部的家庭旅行。我期待這次旅行成為我一生中最美妙的經歷之一。然而，我不久就發現自己的希望被現實的狂風吹得支離破碎，以及一陣痛苦的失望。

　　搭飛機之前，我非常高興，滿心歡喜地等待出發的那一天。那天終於來到我面前。滿懷著期待，我們一家在航班起飛幾個小時前就開始辦理登機手續。辦理登機報到後，我們等了很久，預測著地球另一端會發生的事情。終於，時間到了，我們都登上了飛機。這是我長久以來第一次體驗到坐飛機。爸媽叫我睡覺，但我幾乎無法閉上眼睛，看著半空中壯麗的景色，使我的睡眠時間減少。自然而然地，我沒意識到時間經過，而當飛機抵達時，我已經筋疲力盡了。由於時差很大，我的家人也很疲憊。儘管如此，導遊還是來了，而旅行馬上就開始了。我們搭乘冗長的旅遊巴士，開始了我們的旅程。

　　夏天烈日炎炎，而巴士上沒有遮蔭。我準備的大部分衣服是短袖，所以我意料之外地曬日光浴到天黑。巴士經常停下來，而我們被告知要進入一些景點。但在悶熱的氣溫下，我甚至很難睜開眼睛看建築物。我開始後悔計畫這次旅行。我深入看我的家人，想知道是否只有我那樣想。媽媽似乎也和我一樣疲憊不堪。爸爸和哥哥比我們稍好一些，但也相差不大。當我們前往餐廳吃晚飯時，我很慶幸一天的行程終於結束了。晚餐後，我們全都快速地前往飯店，深深地入睡了。

第二天早上，我還是有時差，但狀態好多了。現在，我的眼睛開始看到周圍的景色。我看見的只是一個大城鎮，和韓國沒有多大的差別。我本來期待在旅行前根本無法想像、非常特別的東西，但結果證明是錯的。唯獨新奇的是一些歷史遺跡與自然遺產，但我對它們沒那麼感興趣。我想要的是類似於電影中的高科技城市。

在美國的十天很快就過去了，主要是因為我在巴士上睡覺。回家後，我令人沮喪的是，將近一半的暑假就這樣消失了，而沒有任何難忘的片刻。在這次失敗之後，我開始不喜歡出國旅行。這種情況一直持續到三年後，我的家人安排新加坡之旅為止。

Step 5. 修正與編輯

初稿終於完成了。下一個階段則是取得對於初稿的回饋意見，並且進行修正。這時候，應該確認文章的前後承接是否自然流暢、句子是否明確而不會太長、拼字與文法是否正確等等。

在英文寫作課中，回饋意見大致分為兩種。第一種是人的回饋（Human Feedback）。人的回饋就是不靠人工智慧或機器，而是真人實際閱讀文章後，綜合判斷文章的優缺點，並提出可供改善的意見。人的回饋可以由同學或老師提供，其中能夠讓自己得知文章在同學眼中看起來如何的同儕回饋（Peer Feedback）特別重要。請務必透過同儕回饋，確認同學是否能理解文章中使用的句子結構或邏輯，而如果不能的話，就需要修改。

下圖是同學閱讀敏奎的文章後給他的同儕回饋。我們英文寫作課的同儕回饋是透過微軟的 Teams app 共用檔案進行。首先三人一組，在共用頻道上傳自己的文章草稿。然後閱讀同學上傳的文章，以註解的方式分享對於文章各方面的意見，包括整體的感想、文章或句子的風格、文法或單字修正的建議等等。

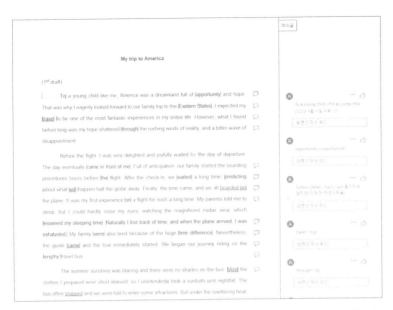

在微軟Teams 的共用頻道上進行的同儕回饋

第二種回饋則是藉由人工智慧工具獲得的 AI 回饋（AI Feedback）。AI 回饋是指用人工智慧技術分析寫好的文章，確認文法、拼字、表達等方面的錯誤，並且取得改善方式的建議。我們的英文寫作課使用 ChatGPT 與 Grammarly 來獲取回饋意見。如同之前我們在段落寫作部分看過的一樣，短文寫作也可以直接把完成的文章輸入 ChatGPT，用各種提示詞來獲得回饋意見。用這個方式，可以把句子修改成正確的文法，或者藉由選擇多種單字，使文章更生動。另外，也可以運用連接詞，使文章更有一體感，或者改變文章的氣氛，使它更正式或流暢。在寫作的最後階段，我們也會用 Grammarly 來檢查文法錯誤與拼字、標點符號。

在這個過程要注意的重點是，從 AI 的回饋取得的修正事項，最後是否要實際用在文章上，取決於寫作者本人。如果 ChatGPT 改變的表達方式不符合自己的意圖，或者修改得太多而減少了文章的獨創性，就不能把回饋意見照單全收。挑選適合自己文章的回饋意見，是我們必須具備的能力。在 ChatGPT 回饋與修正之後，一定要自己實際檢視並修整文章內容，使文章完全成為自己的作品。

接下來，我們看看敏奎如何用 ChatGPT 修正文章。敏奎希望在保持文章整體結構的同時，用最少的修改來提高文章整體的可讀性，並且使前後承接更流暢，所以輸入了以下提示詞。

Prompt

This is a five paragraph descriptive essay. Make slight changes to make the essay more readable and well-flowed. Make sure the overall structure of the essay stays the same, and try to make as few changes as you can.

這是有五個段落的記敘文。請稍作改動，使文章更易讀且流暢。確保文章的整體結構相同，儘量少做修改。

My Trip to America

(2nd draft)

As a young child, I was captivated by the idea of America as a dreamland of opportunities and hope. I eagerly looked forward to our family trip to the East Coast, expecting it to be one of the most fantastic experiences in my entire life. However, reality hit me hard and shattered my hope, leaving me bitterly disappointed.

On the day of departure, I was filled with excitement and anticipation as our family began the boarding procedures hours before our flight. After the check-in, we waited for a long time, thinking about what would happen half the globe away. Finally, we boarded the plane, and despite my parents' advice to sleep, I found myself mesmerized by the stunning aerial view, making it difficult to sleep. My family were also tired because of the huge jet lag. Exhausted upon arrival, the jet lag only added to our fatigue. Nevertheless, the tour guide arrived, and we immediately began our journey on the travel bus.

The sweltering summer heat made the bus ride unbearable, and the lack of shade meant I unintendedly sunbathed until nightfall, since the clothes I packed were mostly short-sleeved. I regretted planning the trip as we stopped at various attractions, unable to open my eyes and appreciate the scenery due to the heat. Looking around, my family was just exhausted as me. After dinner, we were all grateful that the daily schedule finally ended, so we could head to the hotel for much-needed rest.

The next morning, with a better night's sleep and a more refreshed mind, I started to notice the scenery around me. However, what I found was disappointing, as the city was not much different with my hometown in Korea. The buildings looked similar, and the landscape was also nothing special. What I expected was a high-tech city similar to those in the movies, but the only things new were some historical sites and natural heritages which I was not interested.

Despite the ten days passing quickly, it felt like a blur since I slept most of the time on the bus. I returned home feeling depressed, with almost half of the summer vacation gone without any memorable moments. As a result, I developed a dislike for traveling abroad, which lasted until three years later when my family scheduled a trip to Singapore.

我的美國之旅

（二稿）

　　小時候，我就被美國這個充滿機會和希望的夢幻國度深深吸引。我熱切地期盼全家去東岸旅行，期待這次旅行成為我一生中最美妙的經歷之一。然而，現實給了我重重一擊，粉碎了我的希望，讓我失望至極。

　　出發那天，當我們一家人在航班起飛幾個小時前就開始辦理登機手續的時候，我滿懷興奮與期待。辦理登機報到後，我們等了很久，想著地球另一端會發生的事情。終於，我們登上了飛機，儘管爸媽勸我睡覺，但我發現自己被迷人的空中景色迷住了，難以入睡。我的家人也因為巨大的時差而很疲憊。我們抵達時筋疲力盡，而時差更加重我們的疲勞。儘管如此，導遊還是來了，我們馬上就搭乘旅遊巴士開始旅程。

　　悶熱的夏天使得乘坐巴士讓人難以忍受，而缺少遮蔭意味著我意料之外地曬太陽到天黑，因為我打包的衣服大多是短袖。我們停下來造訪各種景點的時候，我後悔計畫了這次旅行，因為天氣熱讓我無法睜開眼睛欣賞風景。環顧四周，家人也和我一樣疲憊。晚餐後，我們都很慶幸一天的行程終於結束了，可以前往飯店，獲得我們非常需要的休息。

　　第二天早上，因為睡了比較好的一覺，精神也比較振奮，所以我開始注意到周圍的景色。然而，我所看到的令人失望，因為那座城市和我在韓國的家鄉沒有多大的差別。建築物看起來很類似，風景也沒什麼特別的。我期待的是類似於電影中的高科技城市，但唯獨新奇的是我並不感興趣的一些歷史遺跡與自然遺產。

　　儘管十天很快就過去了，感覺卻很模糊，因為我在巴士上大部分時間都在睡。回家後我感到很沮喪，因為暑假過了將近一半，卻沒有任何難忘的片刻。結果，我對出國旅行產生了反感，這種反感一直持續到三年後家人安排新加坡之旅為止。

　　敏奎以同學與 ChatGPT 的回饋意見為基礎，修改自己的文章（用顏色標示的部分是和初稿不同的地方），完成了二稿。不過，瀏覽了二稿之後，他認為必須再稍作修改，使文章更符合自己要表達的想法。這是因為，雖然二稿比一開始來得好，但邏輯與表達方式還有略顯模糊的部分。所以，他再次細讀這篇文章並修改，在這個過程中對正文的三個部分做進一步的修改（用顏色標示的是在 ChatGPT 修改後又改過的部分）。

　　首先，他修改第二段，用比較富含感情的方式描寫一家人搭飛機之後疲勞的情況。

Paragraph 2

Finally, we boarded the plane, and despite my parents' advice to sleep, I found myself mesmerized by the stunning aerial view, making it difficult to sleep. My family were also tired because of the huge jet lag. Exhausted upon arrival, the jet lag only added to our fatigue. Nevertheless, the tour guide arrived, and we immediately began our journey on the travel bus.

▼

Paragraph 2

Finally, we boarded the plane, and despite my parents' advice to sleep, I found myself mesmerized by the stunning aerial view that sleeping became impossible. My family was also tired because of the huge jet lag. As a result, after the plane landed, we were all completely drained and staggered like zombies. Nevertheless, the tour guide arrived, and we immediately began our journey on the travel bus.

接下來，他在第三段沒有採用 ChatGPT 所建議的分詞構句（Looking around, my family...），而是使用連接詞，使句子顯得比較簡單（As I looked around, my family...），讓讀者更容易理解。在另一句，他也用 so ~ that 明確表達句子裡的因果關係。

Paragraph 3

The sweltering summer heat made the bus ride unbearable, and the lack of shade meant I unintendedly sunbathed until nightfall, since the clothes I packed were mostly short-sleeved. I regretted planning the trip as we stopped at various attractions, unable to open my eyes and appreciate the scenery due to the heat. Looking around, my family was just exhausted as me. After dinner, we were all grateful that the daily schedule finally ended, so we could head to the hotel for much-needed rest.

Paragraph 3

The sweltering summer heat made the bus ride

unbearable, and the absence of shade caused me to unintentionally get sunburned until nightfall **due to my mostly** short-sleeved clothing. The heat was so intense that I couldn't even open my eyes to appreciate the scenery. Naturally, I started to regret coming on the trip. As I looked around, my family was just as exhausted as I was. **After dinner, we were all grateful that the daily schedule had finally ended so we could head to the hotel for much-needed rest.**

第四段也做了下面的修改，對於旅行第二天的期望－失望，更詳細地說明情境與當時的感覺。

Paragraph 4

The next morning, with a better night's sleep and a more refreshed mind, I started to notice the scenery around me. However, what I found was disappointing, as the city was not much different with my hometown in Korea. The buildings looked similar, and the landscape was also nothing special. What I expected was a high-tech city similar to those in the movies, but the only things new were some historical sites and natural heritages which I was not interested.

▼

Paragraph 4

The next morning, with a better night's sleep and a more refreshed mind, I started to notice the scenery around me. What I had envisioned before the trip was a technologically advanced metropolis reminiscent of the futuristic cities in science fiction films, with towering skyscrapers adorned with vibrant neon lights. However, what I found was disappointing, as the city was not much different from my hometown in Korea. The buildings and roads looked similar, and the landscape was nothing special, either. Even the store brands on the street were the same. The only new things were historical sites and natural heritages that didn't interest me.

而在最後一段，原本的結尾是「我對出國旅行的反感一直持續到三年後的新加坡之旅為止」，修改的版本則是增加從這次旅行學到的教訓（「不要抱太大期待，而是以更開放而實際的心態去旅行」）。

Paragraph 5

Despite the ten days passing quickly, it felt like a blur since I slept most of the time on the bus. I returned home feeling depressed, with almost half of the summer vacation gone without any memorable moments. As a result, I developed a dislike for traveling abroad, which lasted until three years later when my family scheduled a trip to Singapore.

Paragraph 5

The ten days in America passed quickly as I slept most of the time on the bus. **After I returned home, I was very depressed that almost half of the summer vacation was gone without any memorable moments.** In conclusion, my trip to the East Coast taught me a valuable lesson about expectations. Looking back at the experience, I realized that my expectations were too high, so I set myself up for disappointment. Since then, I have approached every trip with a more open and realistic mindset, which has led to more enjoyable and fulfilling experiences three years later in Singapore.

透過同學與 ChatGPT 的回饋意見，他完成了第二份草稿，而在自己細讀過後，又改出第三份草稿。現在只剩下最後階段了。

Step 6. 撰寫最終版本

終於到了最後的階段。在這個階段，要再次確認到目前為止參考回饋意見修改而成的草稿，並且交出最終的稿件。這時候，應該對文章做最後的細讀，檢查錯字、文法、邏輯、表達方式，並思考是否有更好的寫法。而這個時候，Grammarly 之類幫忙檢查文法錯誤、拼字、標點符號的應用程式特別有用。敏奎將第三份草稿輸入 Grammarly，進行最後的檢查。在程式提供的各種建議（13 suggestions）中，他接受了包括替換單字與標點符號錯誤在內的五項小修正，而完成了最終版本。這時候，重點在於不必全盤接受程式建議的各種修正。當然，錯字和標點符

用Grammarly進行文章的最後修正階段

號之類的修正建議應該接受才對，但對於詞語或表達方式的修改，則應該仔細考慮修改過的詞語或表達方式是否適合自己的文章。

　　敏奎的記敘文終於完成了。請比較下面的完成版本和初稿之間有了怎樣的改變，又有多大的改善。

My Trip to America

(final)

As a young child, I was captivated by the idea of America as a dreamland of opportunities and hope. I eagerly looked forward to our family trip to the East Coast, expecting it to be one of the most fantastic experiences of my entire life. However, reality hit me hard and shattered my hopes, leaving me disappointed.

On the day of departure, I was filled with excitement and anticipation as our family began the boarding procedures hours before our flight. After the check-in, we waited for a long time, thinking about what would happen halfway around the world. Finally, we boarded the plane, and despite my parents' advice to sleep, I found myself mesmerized by the stunning aerial view that sleeping became impossible. My family was also tired because of the huge jet lag. As a result, after the plane landed, we were all completely drained and staggered like zombies. Nevertheless, the tour guide arrived, and we immediately began our journey on the travel bus.

The intense summer heat during the bus ride made it unbearable, and the absence of shade caused me to unintentionally get sunburned until nightfall due to my mostly short-sleeved clothing. The heat was so intense that I couldn't even open my eyes to appreciate the scenery. Naturally, I started to regret coming on the trip. As I looked around, my family was just as exhausted as I was. After dinner, we were all grateful that the daily schedule had finally ended so that we could head to the hotel for much-needed rest.

The following day, with a better night's sleep and a more refreshed mind, I started to notice the scenery around me. What I had envisioned before the trip was a technologically advanced metropolis reminiscent of the futuristic cities in science fiction films, with towering skyscrapers adorned with vibrant neon lights. However, what I found was disappointing, as the city was not much different from my hometown in Korea. The buildings and roads looked similar, and the landscape was nothing special, either. Even the store brands on the street were the same. The only new things were historical sites and natural heritages that didn't interest me.

The ten days in America passed quickly as I slept most of the time on the bus. After I returned home, I was very depressed that almost half of the summer vacation was gone without any memorable moments. In conclusion, my trip to the East Coast taught me a valuable lesson about expectations. Looking back at the experience, I realized that my expectations were too high, so I set myself up for disappointment. Since then, I have approached every trip with a more open and realistic mindset, which has led to more enjoyable and fulfilling experiences three years later in Singapore.

我的美國之旅

（最終版）

　　小時候，我就被美國這個充滿機會和希望的夢幻國度深深吸引。我熱切地期盼全家去東岸旅行，期待這次旅行成為我一生中最美妙的經歷之一。然而，現實給了我重重一擊，粉碎了我的希望，讓我感到失望。

　　出發那天，當我們一家人在航班起飛前幾個小時就開始辦理登機手續的時候，我滿懷興奮與期待。辦理登機報到後，我們等了很久，想著世界另一端會發生的事情。終於，我們登上了飛機，儘管爸媽勸我睡覺，但我發現自己被迷人的空中景色迷住了，根本無法入睡。我的家人也因為巨大的時差而很疲憊。結果，飛機著陸後，我們全都筋疲力盡，像行屍走肉一樣踉踉蹌蹌。儘管如此，導遊還是來了，我們馬上就搭乘旅遊巴士開始旅程。

　　乘坐巴士時，夏天的酷暑讓旅程難以忍受，而缺少遮蔭造成我無意間被曬傷，直到入夜為止，因為我的衣服大多是短袖。天氣非常熱，使得我甚至張不開眼睛欣賞風景。自然而然地，我開始後悔來參加這次旅行。環顧四周，家人也和我一樣疲憊。晚餐後，我們都很慶幸一天的行程終於結束了，讓我們能前往飯店，獲得我們非常需要的休息。

第二天，因為睡了比較好的一覺，精神也比較振奮，所以我開始注意周圍的景色。旅行前，我想像的是科技先進的大都市，讓人想起科幻電影中的未來城市，高聳的摩天大樓點綴著鮮豔的霓虹燈。然而，我所看到的令人失望，因為那座城市和我在韓國的家鄉沒有多大的差別。建築物和道路看起來很類似，風景也沒什麼特別的。就連街上的商店品牌也都一樣。唯獨新奇的是我並不感興趣的歷史遺跡與自然遺產。

在美國的十天很快就過去了，因為我在巴士上大部分時間都在睡。回家後我感到非常沮喪，因為暑假過了將近一半，卻沒有任何難忘的片刻。總之，東岸旅行為我上了關於「期望」的寶貴一課。回顧這次經歷，我意識到自己的期望太高，才會讓自己失望。從那以後，我以更加開放而現實的心態對待每一次旅行，這讓我三年後在新加坡有了比較愉快而充實的經歷。

描述文（Descriptive Essay）：智允的寫作

第二部分要看的是智允撰寫描述文的過程。

Step 1. 選定主題

描述文正如其名，是詳細描述事物、場景、人物、情感等等的寫作形式，主要詳細描述經由各種感官經驗感受到的深刻情景，或特定對象的樣貌、特徵、特殊氣味、聲音、顏色等等，讓讀者能夠產生鮮明的想像。雖然與記敘文類似，但記敘文是以自身經驗為基礎，將故事發展下去，而描述文則是著重於詳細描述對象的特徵或外貌、獨特的個性等等。首先，智允用下面的提示詞請 ChatGPT 推薦適合寫成描述文的主題。

Prompt

Recommend good topics for a descriptive essay.

請推薦適合寫成描述文的主題。

Certainly! Here are some additional topic ideas for a descriptive essay:

1. A Childhood Memory: Describe a vivid memory from your childhood that has stayed with you over the years.

2. A Place: Choose a place that you know well, such as your hometown, a park, or a coffee shop, and describe it in detail.

3. A Person: Select someone who has had a significant impact on your life, and describe their appearance, personality, and mannerisms.

4. A Season: Write about your favorite season and describe the sights, sounds, and sensations that make it special to you.

5. A Work of Art: Choose a painting, sculpture, or other piece of art that you find particularly captivating, and describe it in detail.

6. A Sporting Event: Describe the experience of attending a sporting event, such as a baseball game or a football match, from the sights and sounds to the emotions of the crowd.

7. A Pet: Describe a beloved pet, including their appearance, personality, and unique quirks.

8. A Special Occasion: Write about a special occasion, such as a wedding or a birthday party, and describe the atmosphere, decorations, and other details that made it memorable.

I hope these ideas help inspire your writing!

當然！以下是一些額外的描述文主題構想：

1. 一個童年回憶：描述多年來一直伴隨著你的一段童年生動回憶。

2. 一個地方：選擇一個你熟悉的地方，例如家鄉、公園或咖啡館，並詳細描述它。

3. 一個人：選擇對你的人生產生了重大影響的人，描述他們的外貌、個性與習性。

4. 一個季節：描寫你最喜歡的季節，描述它之所以讓你感到特別的視覺、聽覺與感覺。

5. 一件藝術品：選擇一件你認為特別吸引人的繪畫、雕塑或其他藝術作品，並且詳細描述。

6. 一場體育賽事：描述參加體育賽事的經歷，例如棒球賽或（美式）足球賽，包括視覺、聽覺到群眾的情緒等等。

7. 一隻寵物：描述一隻心愛的寵物，包括外表、性格和獨特的怪癖。

8. 一個特殊場合：描寫一個特殊場合，例如婚禮或生日派對，並且描述它令人難忘的氣氛、裝飾與其他細節。

希望這些構想有助於啟發您的寫作！

Step 2. 思考構想

智允在思考過後，選擇了 ChatGPT 建議的場所描述（2. A Place: Choose a place that you know well, such as your hometown, a park, or a coffee shop, and describe it in detail）。她也決定描述她在學校最喜歡、度過最多時間的地方，也就是校內的圖書館。因為一時之間不知該怎麼開始、從哪裡開始描寫圖書館，所以她用以下提示詞尋求幫助。

Prompt

👤 I am writing a descriptive essay about my favorite place – the school library. Can you brainstorm some ideas using a mind map?

我正在寫一篇關於自己最愛的地方 —— 學校圖書館 —— 的描述文。你能用心智圖腦力激盪出一些構想嗎？

💮 Absolutely, here is a mind map with some brainstorming ideas for your descriptive essay about your favorite place, the school library:

當然，以下是一張心智圖，裡面為你關於自己最愛的地方，也就是學校圖書館的描述文，提供了一些腦力激盪的構想：

My Favorite Place: The School Library	**我最喜歡的地方：** 學校圖書館
Appearance —Rows of bookshelves —Comfortable seating —Soft lighting —Large windows —Quiet atmosphere	**外觀** —一排排書架 —舒適的座位 —柔和的燈光 —大窗戶 —安靜的氛圍
Smells —The scent of books —Freshly cleaned carpets —The aroma of coffee	**氣味** —書香 —剛清洗過的地毯 —咖啡香
Sounds —The rustling of pages turning —The soft clicking of computer keys —The sound of whispered conversations	**聲音** —書頁翻動的沙沙聲 —電腦按鍵的輕微嗒嗒聲 —低聲交談的聲音
Feelings —Peaceful —Calming —Cozy —Focused	**感覺** —寧靜 —令人平靜 —舒適 —專注
Activities —Studying —Reading —Writing —Researching	**活動** —學習 —閱讀 —寫作 —研究

People
－Students working individually
－Small study groups
－Teachers offering help
－Librarians checking out books

Benefits
－Improved academic performance
－Expanded knowledge base
－Relaxation and stress relief
－Community building

人
－單獨學習的學生
－小型學習小組
－提供幫助的教師
－辦理書籍出借的圖書館員

益處
－提升學業表現
－擴大知識基礎
－放鬆及緩解壓力
－社群建立

　　心智圖（Mind Map）是指以主題為中心，將聯想到的各種想法畫成開展的樹枝一般的圖。尤其在寫作或整理想法的時候，這是一項很有用的工具。請 ChatGPT 製作描述圖書館的心智圖之後，得到以上的回應。在寫描述文的時候，應該使用具體而細膩的表達方式，也就是描寫對象的顏色、樣貌、氣味、聲音、觸感等感官特質。ChatGPT 以心智圖的形式提出了各種構想，包括圖書館的外觀、氣味、聲音、感覺，以及圖書館裡的人在做什麼、在圖書館可以得到的好處等等。

　　這樣一來，對於文章裡要寫什麼應該稍微有點感覺了。但還有一個問題。要精準描述圖書館，需要使用許多形容詞、副詞之類的詞語，但要寫文章的時候，一時之間可能想不出來。於是智允又用下面的提示詞向 ChatGPT 尋求幫助。

I am writing a descriptive essay about my favorite place - the school library. Can you recommend some descriptive words (including adjectives, adverbs, phrases) that vividly describe the library's appearance, smells, sounds, feelings, activities, people, and benefits?

我正在寫一篇關於自己最愛的地方 —— 學校圖書館——的描述文。你能推薦我一些可以生動描述圖書館外觀、氣味、聲音、感覺、活動、人物與好處的描述性詞語（包含形容詞、副詞、片語）嗎？

Absolutely! Here are some descriptive words and phrases that can help bring your favorite place, the school library, to life in your descriptive essay:

當然！以下是一些在描述文中有助於將您最愛的地方，也就是圖書館，變得栩栩如生的描述性詞彙與片語：

Appearance（外觀）：

Brightly lit	燈光明亮
Cozy nooks	舒適的角落
Inviting atmosphere	吸引人的氛圍
Clean and organized	整潔有序
Rows of bookshelves	一排排的書架
Comfortable seating	舒適的座位
Large windows	寬大的窗戶
Peaceful ambiance	寧靜的氛圍
Modern design	現代設計
Rustic charm	鄉村韻味

Smells（氣味）：

Freshly brewed coffee	現煮咖啡
Aroma of books	書香
Clean and fresh air	清新的空氣
Pleasant scents of flowers	怡人的花香
Hint of wood polish	淡淡的護木油味道
Fragrant candles	芬芳的蠟燭

Sounds（聲音）：

Soft whispers	輕聲細語
Pages turning	翻動的書頁
Hushed footsteps	輕輕的腳步聲
Faint clicking of computer keys	微弱的電腦鍵盤嗒嗒聲
Rustling of papers	紙張的沙沙聲
Melodic chimes of clocks	優美的鐘聲
Quiet background music	安靜的背景音樂
Distant sounds of the school bell	悠遠的上課鈴聲

Feelings（感覺）：

Serenity and calmness	寧靜與平和
Focus and concentration	專注與集中
Inspiration and creativity	靈感與創造力
Comfort and familiarity	舒適與熟悉感
Relaxation and rejuvenation	放鬆與恢復活力
Intellectual stimulation	智性的刺激
Connectedness and community	聯繫感與社區
Pride and accomplishment	自豪與成就感
Satisfaction and fulfillment	滿足與成就感

Activities（活動）：

Studying	學習
Reading	閱讀
Writing	寫作
Researching	研究
Collaborating	協作
Brainstorming	腦力激盪
Reflecting	反思
Learning	學習
Exploring	探索
Experimenting	實驗

People（人物）：

Quiet and studious students	安靜而好學的學生
Curious and knowledgeable researchers	好奇心強、知識淵博的研究者
Friendly and helpful librarians	友好而樂於助人的圖書館員
Engaged and enthusiastic teachers	投入而熱情的教師
Diverse and open-minded community	多元且思想開放的社群

Supportive and collaborative classmates	支持與合作的同學
Focused and driven learners	專注而有動力的學習者
Creative and innovative thinkers	有創意且創新的思考者

Benefits（好處）：

- Access to vast resources and information	一獲取大量資源與資訊
- Enhanced academic performance	一提高學業表現
- Improved critical thinking and problem-solving skills	一促進批判性思維與解決問題的能力
- Expanded knowledge and understanding	一擴展知識與理解能力
- Opportunity for professional and personal growth	一專業及個人成長的機會
- Stimulated curiosity and creativity	一激發好奇心與創造力
- Reduced stress and anxiety	一減輕壓力與焦慮
- Encouragement of lifelong learning and self-improvement	一鼓勵終身學習與自我增進
- Building of lasting relationships and connections	一建立持久的關係與聯繫

I hope these descriptive words and phrases inspire your descriptive essay about the school library and bring the place to life for your readers!

希望這些描述性詞彙和片語能為你關於學校圖書館的描述文帶來靈感，並且讓讀者感到這個地方栩栩如生！

Step 3. 撰寫大綱

　　經過以上步驟，描述圖書館的寫作題材與材料（單字與表達方式等）已經準備好了。智允以這些為基礎建立了大綱，作為文章的架構。在這個階段，她用下面的提示詞幫助自己制定大綱。

Prompt

👤 I am writing a 5 paragraph descriptive essay about my favorite place – the school library. Write an essay outline.

我正在寫一篇關於自己最愛的地方 —— 學校圖書館 —— 的五段描述文。撰寫一份文章的大綱。

💬 Sure, here's an outline for your 5-paragraph descriptive essay about your favorite place, the school library:

I. Introduction
-Start with an attention-grabbing hook that introduces the topic of your essay.
-Provide a brief overview of the school library and

its significance to you.

-End with a thesis statement that highlights the key aspects of the library that you will describe in the essay.

II. Appearance

-Describe the physical appearance of the library, including the rows of bookshelves, comfortable seating, soft lighting, large windows, and quiet atmosphere.

-Use sensory language to paint a vivid picture of the library's appearance.

III. Smells and Sounds

-Describe the unique smells and sounds of the library, including the scent of books, freshly cleaned carpets, aroma of coffee, rustling of pages turning, soft clicking of computer keys, and whispered conversations.

-Use descriptive language to convey the atmosphere and sensory experiences of the library.

IV. Feelings and Activities

-Describe the feelings and activities that the library evokes, including a sense of peacefulness, calmness, coziness, and focus, as well as studying, reading, writing, and researching.

-Use specific examples and anecdotes to illustrate these feelings and activities.

V. Benefits and Conclusion

-Describe the benefits of spending time in the library, including improved academic performance, expanded knowledge base, relaxation and stress relief, and community building.

-Summarize the key points of the essay and restate the thesis statement.

-End with a concluding statement that leaves a lasting impression on the reader.

I hope this outline helps you organize your thoughts and ideas for your descriptive essay about your favorite place, the school library!

當然，以下是關於你最愛的地方，也就是學校圖書館的五段描述文大綱：

I. 前言
－從引人注意的引言開始，介紹你的文章主題。
－簡要介紹學校圖書館，以及它對你的意義。
－以主旨陳述結尾，強調你將在文章中描述的圖書館主要方面。

II. 外觀
－描述圖書館的外觀，包括一排排的書架、舒適的座位、柔和的燈光、寬大的窗戶和安靜的氛圍。
－使用感官語言，生動地描繪圖書館的外觀。

III. 氣味和聲音
－描述圖書館獨特的氣味與聲音，包括書香、剛清洗過的地毯、咖啡的香味、翻動書頁的沙沙聲、電腦按鍵的輕微嗒嗒聲以及低聲交談。
－使用描述性語言，傳達圖書館的氛圍與感官體驗。

IV. 感覺與活動
－描述圖書館喚起的感覺與活動，包括寧靜、平和、

舒適、專注的感覺，以及學習、閱讀、寫作和研
究。

－用具體的例子和軼事來說明這些感受和活動。

V. 好處與結論

－描述花時間在圖書館的好處，包括改善學業表
現、擴大知識基礎、放鬆與緩解壓力，以及社群
建立。

－總結文章要點，重新進行主旨陳述。

－最後寫下帶給讀者深刻印象的結語。

　　希望這份大綱能幫助你整理思考與想法，寫出關於
自己最愛的地方，也就是學校圖書館的描述文！

Step 4. 撰寫草稿

　　智允在 Step 3 透過 ChatGPT 的幫助，完成了圖書館
的描述文大綱。而在這個階段，就要將大綱具體化為文章
了。如同之前在撰寫記敘文的過程中提到的，在擬定草稿
的階段，嚴格禁止學生使用 ChatGPT 或 Google 翻譯等 AI
工具，因為這個階段必須完全專注於自己的寫作。智允同
樣參考了一些題材與完成的大綱，寫好了描述文的草稿。

The School Library

(1st draft)

Everyone has their favorite place. It may be a place to meet friends, a place to rest, or a place that holds precious memories. After attending Seoul Science High School for two and a half years, I think I can say firmly that my favorite place here is the school library. The library has always been a great place to rest, and the recent renovations have only made the place better. I will tell three reasons why the library is my favorite place and present the serene beauty of the fountain of knowledge.

Firstly, the library offers a unique interior that cannot be found anywhere in the school. When you step through the glass doors, you are met with a wide area with comfortable chairs, decorative plants, and a long desk where students usually sit to study. One wall is covered with books, and another has a large window, of which the sunlight comes in through. The left wall has transparent sliding doors which lead the way to the many rows of books. Between the books are places to study and rest. Overall, it offers a great environment for both studying and relaxing.

Secondly, coupled with the unique interior, the smells and sounds also take part in making the environment appealing. The scent of books is prevalent all over the library, while the sound of people typing on their laptops, the sound of turning pages, and whispered conversations can be heard now and then. These all make for a very peaceful and relaxing environment. There are not so many places in the school where you can relax quietly like this, so it is a major upside.

Finally, the library is a perfect place to do your work. As stated above, the library is one of the most quiet, peaceful places in school. If you want to concentrate on studying, but don't feel like going to the dormitory, this is the place of your choice. Also, you have access to the countless books listed in the bookshelves. Whenever you feel like you want to read a literature work, a book about world history, or research expert information using recent books, the library can help you. The library isn't called a fountain of knowledge for nothing, after all.

Spending time in the library is a very good way to improve yourself. You can improve academic performance, expand your knowledge base, and even build small communities. In conclusion, the library is a perfect place to study or relax, and is most definitely my favorite place in Seoul Science High School.

學校圖書館

（初稿）

　　每個人都有自己最愛的地方。可能是和朋友見面的地方，可能是休息的地方，也可能是有著珍貴回憶的地方。在首爾科學高中就讀兩年半之後，我想我可以肯定地說，我在這裡最喜歡的地方是學校圖書館。圖書館一直都是休息的好地方，而最近的翻修更是讓這裡變得更好。我將講述圖書館之所以是我最喜歡的地方的三個原因，並展現這座知識泉源的寧靜之美。

　　第一，圖書館提供全校獨一無二的內部裝潢。當你走過玻璃門，會見到一個寬闊的區域，裡面有舒適的椅子、裝飾性的植物和一張長桌，學生通常會坐在那裡學習。有一面牆擺滿了書，另一面牆則有大窗戶，陽光從窗戶照進來。左邊的牆壁有透明的推拉門，通往許多排的書。在書之間是學習與休息的地方。整體而言，這裡為學習與放鬆提供很好的環境。

第二，除了獨特的內部裝潢，氣味與聲音也共同扮演使環境吸引人的角色。圖書館裡到處彌漫著書香，同時還能不時聽到人們用筆記型電腦打字的聲音、翻動書頁的聲音，以及低聲交談聲。這些都營造出一個非常寧靜且放鬆的環境。在學校裡，像這樣能讓人安靜放鬆的地方並不多，所以這是一大優點。

最後，這座圖書館是完美的工作場所。如上所述，圖書館是學校裡最安靜祥和的地方之一。如果你想專心學習，但又不想去宿舍，這裡就是你的好選擇。你也可以取用書架上列出的無數書籍。無論何時，只要你想閱讀文學作品、關於世界史的書，或者利用最新書籍研究專家資訊，圖書館都能幫你。畢竟，圖書館被稱為知識泉源不是沒有道理的。

在圖書館度過時光是提升自我很好的方法。你可以改善學業表現、擴大知識基礎，甚至建立小型社群。總之，這座圖書館是學習或放鬆的完美場所，也絕對是我在首爾科學高中最喜歡的地方。

Step 5. 修正與編輯

初稿終於完成了。接下來，智允要藉由同學與 ChatGPT 的回饋意見來修改自己的文章。首先，同學給了智允哪些回饋意見呢？同學稱讚她對圖書館視覺、嗅覺、聽覺方面的描寫，同時也建議她讓整體的表達方式更豐富多樣，並且使用生動的單字，讓文章更有描述文的樣子。此外，同學也指出了不自然的表達方式，以及文法方面錯誤的部分。智允依照同學的回饋意見，修改了自己的文章。而為了讓文章中使用的表達方式更豐富而自然，她也在 ChatGPT 輸入了以下提示詞。為了防止 ChatGPT 把文章直接重寫，她要求把改善的建議一項一項列出來。

Prompt

I will give you a passage. I want you to suggest some changes in vocabulary which will help make it sound more lively. Don't give me a improved passage, list them with 1. 2. 3.

我會給你一篇文章。請建議一些詞彙的變化，讓文章聽起來更生動。請不要直接給我改好的文章，而是以 1、2、3 列出。

Certainly! Here are some suggested changes to make the passage sound more lively:

1. Instead of "Everyone has their favorite place,"

consider using a more engaging phrase like "Each person holds a special haven close to their heart."

2. Instead of "It may be a place to meet friends, a place to rest, or a place that holds precious memories," try "Whether it's a gathering spot for cherished friendships, a sanctuary for solace, or a repository of treasured moments."

3. Instead of "After attending Seoul Science High School for two and a half years," consider "During my enriching journey of two and a half years at Seoul Science High School."

4. Instead of "I think I can say firmly," consider "I can confidently assert."

5. Instead of "the school library," consider "the vibrant hub of knowledge."

6. Instead of "The library has always been a great place to rest," try "The library has forever embraced me in its soothing embrace."

7. Instead of "the recent renovations have only made the place better," consider "the recent renovations have breathed new life into this space of wonder."

8. Instead of "I will tell three reasons why the library is my favorite place," try "Allow me to present three compelling reasons that make the library my ultimate sanctuary."

9. Instead of "the serene beauty of the fountain of knowledge," consider "the awe-inspiring majesty of the wellspring of knowledge."

10. Instead of "Firstly," consider "To begin with."

11. Instead of "offers a unique interior," try "boasts an unparalleled ambiance."

12. Instead of "comfortable chairs," consider "plush seating."

13. Instead of "decorative plants," try "lush greenery."

14. Instead of "long desk," consider "expansive workstations."

15. Instead of "Overall, it offers a great environment," try "All in all, it provides an enchanting milieu."

16. Instead of "the scent of books is prevalent," consider "the aroma of books permeates the air."

17. Instead of "sound of people typing on their laptops," try "keyboard clatter fills the space."

18. Instead of "the sound of turning pages," consider "the gentle rustle of pages turning."

19. Instead of "whispered conversations," try "hushed dialogues."

20. Instead of "a very peaceful and relaxing environment," consider "an oasis of tranquility."

21. Instead of "perfect," use "exquisite" or "impeccable."

22. Instead of "quiet" and "peaceful," use "serene" and "tranquil."

23. Instead of "do your work," use "accomplish your tasks" or "tackle your assignments."

24. Instead of "If you want to concentrate on studying," use "If you crave unwavering focus on your studies."

25. Instead of "countless books," use "an abundance of books" or "a myriad of books."

26. Instead of "feel like," use "have the inclination" or "desire."

27. Instead of "literature work," use "literary masterpiece" or "captivating piece of literature."

28. Instead of "world history," use "epic historical accounts" or "globe-spanning historical narratives."

29. Instead of "research expert information using recent books," use "explore cutting-edge knowledge with the latest books."

30. Instead of "fountain of knowledge," use "epicenter of wisdom" or "font of enlightenment."

31. Instead of "Spending time in the library is a very good way," use "Immersing yourself in the library experience is an excellent means."

32. Instead of "improve yourself," use "elevate your intellectual prowess" or "enhance personal growth."

33. Instead of "academic performance," use "scholastic achievements" or "educational excellence."

34. Instead of "knowledge base," use "intellectual repertoire" or "storehouse of wisdom."

35. Instead of "build small communities," use "forge meaningful connections" or "nurture close-knit bonds."

36. Instead of "perfect place," use "idyllic sanctuary" or "utopian haven."

Feel free to mix and match these suggestions to suit your preference and style.

當然！以下是一些讓這段文章聽起來更生動的修改建議：

1. 與其說「每個人都有自己最愛的地方」，不如考慮使用「每個人心中都有一個特別的避風港」這種比較吸引人的語句。

2. 與其說「可能是和朋友見面的地方，可能是休息的地方，也可能是有著珍貴回憶的地方」，不如試試看「不論它是珍貴友誼的聚會處、心靈慰藉的庇護所，或者珍藏美好時光的寶庫」。

3. 考慮將「在首爾科學高中就讀兩年半之後」改成「在首爾科學高中就讀兩年半的充實旅程中」。

4. 考慮將「我想我可以肯定地說」改成「我可以自信地斷言」。

5. 考慮將「學校圖書館」改成「充滿活力的知識中心」。

6. 與其說「圖書館一直都是休息的好地方」，不如試試看「圖書館永遠用它撫慰的懷抱擁抱著我」。

7. 考慮將「最近的**翻修**更是讓這裡變得更好」改成「最近的**翻修**為這個神奇的空間注入了新的生命」。

8. 與其說「我將講述圖書館之所以是我最喜歡的地方的三個原因」，不如試試看「讓我提出三個令人信服的理由，證明圖書館是我的終極庇護處」。

9. 考慮將「知識泉源的寧靜之美」改成「知識泉源的威嚴」。

10. 考慮將「第一」改成「首先」。

11. 與其說「提供獨特的內部裝潢」，不如試試看「擁有無與倫比的氛圍」。

12. 考慮將「舒適的椅子」改成「絨布座位」。

13. 與其說「裝飾性的植物」，不如試試看「茂盛的綠色植物」。

14. 考慮將「長桌」改成「寬敞的工作區」。

15. 與其說「整體而言，這裡提供很好的環境」，不如試試看「從各方面來說，它提供一個迷人的環境」。

16. 考慮將「書香彌漫」改成「書香彌漫在空氣中」。

17. 與其說「人們用筆記型電腦打字的聲音」，不如試試看「鍵盤的嗒嗒聲充斥在空間中」。

18. 考慮將「翻動書頁的聲音」改成「書頁翻動的沙沙聲」。

19. 與其說「低聲交談」，不如試試看「壓低聲音的對話」。

20. 考慮將「非常寧靜且放鬆的環境」改成「寧靜的綠洲」。

21. 將「完美的」改成「精緻的」或「無可挑剔的」。

22. 將「安靜的」和「祥和的」改成「寧靜的」與「平靜的」。

23. 將「做你的工作」改成「達成你的工作」或「處理你的作業」。

24. 將「如果你想專心學習」改成「如果你渴望堅定不移地專心學習」。

25. 將「無數書籍」改成「豐富的書籍」或「數不盡的書籍」。

26. 將「想要」改成「有意」或「渴望」。

27. 將「文學作品」改成「文學傑作」或「迷人的文學作品」。

28. 將「世界史」改成「史詩般的歷史描述」或「橫

跨全球的歷史敘事」。

29. 將「利用最新書籍研究專家資訊」改成「用最新書籍探索尖端知識」。

30. 將「知識泉源」改成「智慧的中心」或「啟蒙之泉」。

31. 將「在圖書館度過時光是很好的方法」改成「沉浸在圖書館的體驗中是極佳的方式」。

32. 將「提升自我」改成「提高智能」或「促進個人成長」。

33. 將「學業表現」改成「學術成就」或「教育上的卓越」。

34. 將「知識基礎」改成「知識儲備」或「智慧寶庫」。

35. 將「建立小型社群」改成「建立有意義的連結」或「培養緊密的關係」。

36. 將「完美場所」改成「田園般的庇護處」或「烏托邦般的避風港」。

請隨意搭配這些建議，以符合您的偏好與風格。

智允從 ChatGPT 生成的結果中，選擇了文章需要修改的部分，而完成了二稿。下面用顏色標示的部分，就是智允接受 ChatGPT 修改的部分。我們看看二稿和初稿有哪些不同的地方。

The School Library

(2nd draft)

Everyone holds a special place in their hearts. Whether it be a gathering place to meet friends, a place to find solace, or a place that holds precious memories. After the two and a half years at Seoul Science High School, I think I can confidently say that my favorite place here is the school library. The library has always been a great place, and the recent renovations have breathed new life into it. Allow me to present three reasons why the library is my favorite place and introduce the serene beauty of the fountain of knowledge.

To begin with, the library boasts a unique interior that cannot be found anywhere in the school. When you step through the glass doors, you are met with a wide area with plush seating, decorative plants, and a long desk where students usually sit to study. One wall is covered with books, and another has a large window, of which the sunlight comes in through. The left wall has transparent sliding doors which lead the way to the many rows of books. Between the books are places to study and rest. All in all, it provides an enchanting milieu for both studying and relaxing.

Secondly, coupled with the unique interior, the scents and sounds also take part in making the environment appealing. The aroma of books permeates the air, while the sound of people typing on their laptops, the gentle rustling of turning pages, and hushed conversations can be heard now and then. These all make for a tranquil environment. There are not so many places in the school where you can relax quietly like this, so it is a major upside.

Finally, the library is the perfect place to do your work. As stated above, the library is one of the most serene, tranquil places in school. If you want to concentrate on studying, but don't have the inclination to go to the dormitory, this is the place of your choice. Also, you have access to the myriad of books listed in the bookshelves. Whenever you feel like you want to read a literary masterpiece or a book about world history, or explore cutting-edge knowledge using recent books, the library can help you. The library isn't called a fountain of knowledge for nothing, after all.

Immersing yourself in the library is an excellent means to enhance personal growth. You can improve academic performance, expand your knowledge base, and even nurture bonds with new people. It also acts as a sanctuary in which you can seek solace and revitalize. It is most definitely my favorite place in Seoul Science High School.

學校圖書館

（二稿）

每個人心中都有一個特別的地方。不論它是朋友聚會的地方、尋求慰藉的地方，還是有著珍貴回憶的地方。在首爾科學高中就讀的兩年半之後，我想我可以自信地說，我在這裡最喜歡的地方是學校圖書館。圖書館一直都是個好地方，而最近的翻修為它注入了新的生命。讓我提出圖書館之所以是我最喜歡的地方的三個理由，並且介紹這座知識泉源的寧靜之美。

首先，圖書館擁有全校獨一無二的內部裝潢。當你走過玻璃門，會見到一個寬闊的區域，裡面有絨布座位、裝飾性的植物和一張長桌，學生通常會坐在那裡學習。有一面牆擺滿了書，另一面牆則有一扇大窗戶，陽光從窗戶照進來。左邊的牆壁有透明的推拉門，通往許多排的書。在書之間是學習與休息的地方。從各方面來說，它提供一個學習與放鬆的迷人環境。

第二，除了獨特的內部裝潢，香氣與聲音也共同扮演使環境吸引人的角色。書香彌漫在空氣中，同時還能不時聽到人們用筆記型電腦打字的聲音、翻動書頁的沙沙聲，以及壓低聲音的對話。這些都營造出一個寧靜的環境。在學校裡，像這樣能讓人安靜放鬆的地方並不多，所以這是一大優點。

最後，這座圖書館是完美的工作場所。如上所述，圖書館是學校裡最寧靜、安詳的地方之一。如果你想專心學習，但又無意去宿舍，這裡就是你的好選擇。你也可以取用書架上列出的無數書籍。無論何時，只要你想閱讀文學傑作、關於世界史的書，或者利用最新書籍探索尖端知識，圖書館都能幫你。畢竟，圖書館被稱為知識泉源不是沒有道理的。

沉浸於圖書館，是促進個人成長極佳的方式。你可以改善學業表現、擴大知識基礎，甚至和新認識的人培

養關係。它也是可以尋求慰藉、恢復活力的庇護處。它
絕對是我在首爾科學高中最喜歡的地方。

參考 ChatGPT 的回饋意見後，詞彙和表達方式都變得
較為豐富，也更稱得上是一篇描述文了。在結論段落也可
以看到，重新整理了文章的核心概念，使文章的結構更穩
健，也使結尾更令人印象深刻。最後，智允再次細讀二稿
並檢查文章。

Step 6. 撰寫最終版本

完成修改與編輯之後，終於進入了寫作的最後一個階
段。最後，智允用 Grammarly 再次確認錯字、文法、邏
輯、表達方式等等。在 Grammarly 的 25 項修改建議中，智
允接受了包括標點符號與單字替換在內的 6 項，最後又再
次細讀了自己的文章。如此一來，終於完成了描述圖書館
多樣面貌的精彩文章。

The School Library

(final)

Everyone holds a special place in their hearts. Whether it be a gathering place to meet friends, a place to find solace or a place that holds precious memories. After the two and a half years at Seoul Science High School, I think I can confidently say that my favorite place here is the school library. The library has always been a great place, and the recent renovations have breathed new life into it. Allow me to present three reasons why the library is my favorite place and introduce the serene beauty of the fountain of knowledge.

To begin with, the library boasts a unique interior that cannot be found anywhere in the school. When you step through the glass doors, you are met with a wide area with plush seating, decorative plants, and a long desk where students usually sit to study. One wall is covered with books, and another has a large window through which the sunlight comes in. The left wall has transparent sliding doors which lead the way to the many rows of books. Between the books are places to study and rest. All in all, it provides an enchanting milieu for both learning and relaxing.

Secondly, coupled with the unique interior, the scents and sounds also take part in making the environment appealing. The aroma of books permeates the air, while the sound of people typing on their laptops, the gentle rustling of turning pages, and hushed conversations can be heard now and then. These all make for a tranquil environment. There are not so many places in the school where you can relax quietly like this, so it is a major upside.

Finally, the library is the perfect place to do your work. As stated above, the library is one of the most serene, tranquil places in school. If you want to concentrate on studying but don't have the inclination to go to the dormitory, this is the place of your choice. Also, you have access to the myriad of books listed on the bookshelves. Whenever you feel like you want to read a literary masterpiece or a book about world history or explore cutting-edge knowledge using recent books, the library can help you. The library isn't called a fountain of knowledge for nothing, after all.

Immersing yourself in the library is an excellent means to enhance personal growth. You can improve academic performance, expand your knowledge base, and even nurture bonds with new people. It also acts as a sanctuary in which you can seek solace and revitalize. It is most definitely my favorite place in Seoul Science High School.

學校圖書館

（最終版）

每個人心中都有一個特別的地方。不論它是朋友聚會的地方、尋求慰藉的地方，還是有著珍貴回憶的地方。在首爾科學高中就讀的兩年半之後，我想我可以自信地說，我在這裡最喜歡的地方是學校圖書館。圖書館一直都是很棒的地方，而最近的翻修為它注入了新的生命。讓我提出圖書館之所以是我最喜歡的地方的三個理由，並且介紹這座知識泉源的寧靜之美。

首先，圖書館擁有全校獨一無二的內部裝潢。當你走過玻璃門，會見到一個寬闊的區域，裡面有絨布座位、裝飾性的植物和一張長桌，學生通常會坐在那裡學習。有一面牆擺滿了書，另一面牆則有一扇大窗戶，陽光從窗戶照進來。左邊的牆壁有透明的推拉門，通往許多排的書。在書之間是學習與休息的地方。從各方面來說，它提供一個學習與放鬆的迷人環境。

第二，除了獨特的內部裝潢，香氣與聲音也共同扮演使環境吸引人的角色。書香彌漫在空氣中，同時還能不時聽到人們用筆記型電腦打字的聲音、翻動書頁的沙沙聲，以及壓低聲音的對話。這些都營造出一個寧靜的環境。在學校裡，像這樣能讓人安靜放鬆的地方並不多，所以這是一大優點。

最後，這座圖書館是完美的工作場所。如上所述，圖書館是學校裡最寧靜、安詳的地方之一。如果你想專心學習，但又無意去宿舍，這裡就是你的好選擇。你也可以取用書架上列出的無數書籍。無論何時，只要你想閱讀文學傑作、關於世界史的書，或者利用最新書籍探索尖端知識，圖書館都能幫你。畢竟，圖書館被稱為知識泉源不是沒有道理的。

沉浸於圖書館，是促進個人成長極佳的方式。你可以改善學業表現、擴大知識基礎，甚至和新認識的人培養關係。它也是可以尋求慰藉、恢復活力的庇護處。它絕對是我在首爾科學高中最喜歡的地方。

說明文（Expository Essay）：閱材的寫作

第三部分要看的是閱材撰寫說明文的過程。

Step 1. 選定主題

　　說明文的目的是基於對主題的分析與理解，提供明確而具體的資訊。這種文章以客觀的事實與證據來論證主題，因此主要以容易理解而清楚的句子寫成。代表性的說明文類型，有關於兩個主題之間相似點與差異點的比較對照文（Compare and Contrast Essay），以及分析特定主題之原因－結果的因果關係文（Cause and Effect Essay）。在正式進入閱材的寫作過程之前，讓我們先了解一下比較對照文的兩種寫作方式（Point-by-Point, Block Method）。

Point-by-Point Method（逐點比較法）

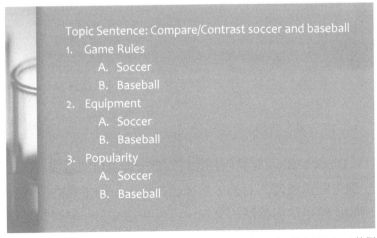

Point-by-Point Method 範例

Point-by-Point Method 是指針對兩個比較對象的特定重點，逐一進行比較的方式。在短文的正文部分，會對每個重點進行兩者之間的比較。如上圖所示，用這個方式比較足球和棒球，可以依照比賽規則、設備、流行程度等重點來比較兩者的共同點與差異，讓讀者能具體比較並了解兩者。Point-by-Point Method 主要用在想強調重要內容或重點間詳細比較的時候。

Block Method（塊狀比較法）

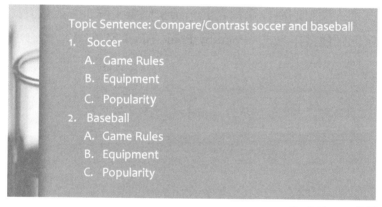

Block Method 範例

Block Method 是將兩個比較對象分成各自的區塊，先對一個主題做整體的討論，然後再討論另一個主題的方式。例如比較足球與棒球的文章，可以在正文第一段討論足球的所有資訊，然後在正文第二段討論棒球的所有資訊，對足球進行比較。這個方法是一次將特定對象的特徵與差異全部寫出來。因為是在讀者完全了解一個主題之後,再討論另一個主題,所以讀者可以把對象區分開來進行比較。

　　接下來,我們來看看因果關係文的兩種寫作法(Focus-on-Cause, Focus-on-Effect)。

Focus-on-Cause(著重於原因的寫法)

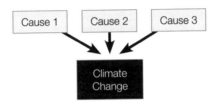

　　Focus-on-Cause 是著重於原因的短文寫作方式。正文部分討論事件的主要原因,以及每個原因如何導致結果。例如關於氣候變遷的 Focus-on-Cause 短文,會將重點放在氣候變遷的原因,在正文的每個段落說明。

Focus-on-Effect(著重於結果的寫法)

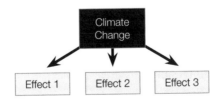

Focus-on-Effect 是著重於結果的短文寫作方式。這種文章的目的是說明特定原因或事件造成的結果。例如關於氣候變遷的 Focus-on-Effect 短文，會將重點放在氣候變遷造成的影響，並且在正文的每個段落一一說明這些影響。

讓我們回到閱材的寫作過程吧。他用下面的提示詞，取得說明文主題的建議。

Prompt

Recommend good topics for a compare and contrast essay.

請推薦適合寫成比較對照文的主題。

Certainly! Here are some good topics for a compare and contrast essay:

-Traditional Education vs. Online Education: Compare and contrast the benefits and drawbacks of traditional classroom learning and online education.

-City Life vs. Country Life: Explore the differences and similarities between living in a bustling city and a peaceful countryside.

-Books vs. Movies: Analyze the advantages and disadvantages of reading books versus watching their film adaptations.

-Democracy vs. Authoritarianism: Compare and contrast the political systems of democratic societies and authoritarian regimes.

-Nature vs. Nurture: Examine the influence of genetics and environment on human development and behavior.

-Renewable Energy vs. Fossil Fuels: Discuss the pros and cons of renewable energy sources (such as solar and wind power) and fossil fuels (like coal and oil).

-Android vs. iOS: Compare and contrast the features, user experience, and ecosystem of Android and iOS operating systems.

-World War I vs. World War II: Explore the causes, impact, and outcomes of these two major global conflicts.

Remember to choose a topic that you find interesting and can gather enough information to support your arguments effectively.

當然！以下是一些適合寫成比較對照文的主題：

－傳統教育與線上教育：比較並對照傳統課堂學習與線上教育的利弊。

－城市生活與鄉村生活：探討生活在繁華都市與寧靜鄉村的異同。

－書籍與電影：分析閱讀書籍與觀看〔書的〕改編電影的利弊。

－民主與專制：比較並對照民主社會與專制政權的政治制度。

－先天與後天：檢視遺傳與環境對人類發展與行為的影響。

－再生能源與化石燃料：討論再生能源（如太陽能與風力）與化石燃料（如煤炭與石油）的利弊。

－Android 與 iOS：比較並對照 Android 與 iOS 作業系統的功能、使用者體驗與生態系。

－第一次世界大戰與第二次世界大戰：探討這兩次重大全球衝突的起因、影響與結果。

切記選擇一個您認為有趣，而且能收集足夠資訊來有效支持論點的主題。

Step 2. 思考構想

閔材瀏覽了一下 ChatGPT 提供的主題清單，大概了解怎樣的主題適合寫成說明文。可惜的是，他對 ChatGPT 推薦的主題沒什麼興趣。所以，他決定用自己喜歡的題材來寫作。閔材最近對攀岩（Climbing）很感興趣，而作為體育競賽的攀登又細分為先鋒攀登（Lead Climbing）、抱石（Bouldering）、速度攀登（Speed Climbing）等種類。很多人知道速度攀登是在指定路線比賽攀登速度，但對於先鋒攀登和抱石比較陌生，容易搞混，所以他決定撰寫比較這兩者的短文。首先，閔材用下面的提示詞，進一步了解攀岩中的先鋒攀登與抱石。

Prompt

What are the differences between Lead and Bouldering?

先鋒攀登與抱石的差別是什麼？

Lead climbing and Bouldering are two distinct forms of rock climbing, differing in several key aspects. Here are the main differences between Lead climbing and Bouldering:

- Height and Rope Usage:

• Lead Climbing: In lead climbing, climbers ascend a taller wall or rock face using a rope. They clip the rope into pre-placed protection points (such as bolts or traditional gear) as they progress upward.

• Bouldering: Bouldering involves climbing shorter routes or "problems" that are typically 10 to 20 feet high, without using a rope. Instead of ropes, climbers rely on crash pads placed beneath the boulder to cushion falls.

- Difficulty and Grading:

• Lead Climbing: In lead climbing, routes are often longer and more varied in terms of difficulty. Climbs can range from relatively easy to extremely challenging, and they are graded on a difficulty scale such as the Yosemite Decimal System (YDS) or the French Scale.

• Bouldering: Bouldering problems are generally shorter but tend to be more physically demanding and technically challenging in a concentrated manner. Bouldering problems are also graded, typically using the V-scale (V0, V1, V2, etc.) or the Fontainebleau grading system.

- Climbing Style and Technique:

• Lead Climbing: Lead climbers must manage the rope, clipping it into protection points as they ascend. They often need to plan their moves strategically, conserve energy, and focus on endurance as they climb longer routes. Lead climbing involves a combination of technical skills, route reading, and stamina.

• Bouldering: Bouldering emphasizes explosive movements, strength, and problem-solving skills in a shorter burst of climbing. Bouldering often requires intricate footwork, dynamic movements, and creative problem-solving to navigate challenging sequences on the rock.

- Risk and Safety:

• Lead Climbing: Due to the higher heights and use of ropes, lead climbing carries a different level of risk. Falling during lead climbing can result in longer falls compared to Bouldering, and the belayer (the person managing the rope) must be attentive to catch potential falls.

• Bouldering: Bouldering is generally considered lower risk in terms of fall height because climbers are closer to the ground. However, Bouldering still carries risks, such as injuries from falling incorrectly or landing on uneven surfaces.

- Equipment:

• Lead Climbing: Lead climbers require additional equipment, including climbing ropes, quickdraws (for clipping into protection points), harnesses, helmets, and belay devices. They may also use traditional climbing gear, such as nuts or cams, depending on the type of climb.

• Bouldering: Bouldering requires minimal equipment. Climbers typically use climbing shoes, chalk to improve grip, and crash pads for protection against falls. Some boulderers may also use brushes to clean holds and improve friction.

It's worth noting that while lead climbing is often done outdoors on natural rock formations, it can also be practiced indoors on artificial climbing walls. Bouldering, on the other hand, can be done both outdoors and indoors, typically on shorter artificial walls or dedicated Bouldering areas.

先鋒攀登與抱石是兩種不同的攀岩形式，在幾個關鍵方面有所不同。以下是先鋒攀登和抱石的主要差異：

－高度與繩索的使用：

• 先鋒攀登：在先鋒攀登中，攀登者用繩索攀登較高的牆面或岩壁。在向上攀爬的過程中，他們會將繩索扣在預先設置的保護點（例如錨栓或傳統裝置）。

• 抱石：抱石是攀登較短的路線（或稱為「problem」），通常 10 至 20 英尺高，不使用繩索。攀登者不依靠繩索，而是靠放置於岩石下的防撞墊來緩衝跌落。

－難度與分級：

• 先鋒攀登：在先鋒攀登中，路線通常較長，難度也較多樣。攀登難度從相對容易到極具挑戰性不等，並根據難度系統（如優勝美地十進位系統（YDS）或法國分級）進行分級。

• 抱石：抱石路線通常較短，但往往對體力要求更高，技術挑戰性也更集中。抱石路線也分等級，通常採用 V 系統（V0、V1、V2 等等）或楓丹白露分級系統。

－攀登風格與技巧：

• 先鋒攀登：從事先鋒攀登者必須管理繩索，在攀登時將繩索扣在保護點上。在攀登較長的路線時，他們往往需要策略性地規劃動作、節省體力並著重於持久力。先鋒攀登涉及技術能力、路線判讀與耐力的綜合運用。

• 抱石：抱石強調較短時間攀爬過程中的爆發性動作、力量與解決問題的技巧。抱石通常需要複雜精細的步法、動態動作與創造性的問題解決方法，才能在岩石上完成具有挑戰性的一連串動作。

－風險與安全：

• 先鋒攀登：由於高度較高並使用繩索，先鋒攀登具有不同程度的風險。與抱石相比，在先鋒攀登時墜落距離可能較長，而確保者（管理繩索的人）必須注意接住可能發生的墜落。

• 抱石：就墜落高度而言，抱石通常被認為風險較低，因為攀登者離地面較近。然而，抱石仍然存在風險，例如不正確的墜落或落在不平的地面上造成受傷。

－裝備：

• 先鋒攀登：從事先鋒攀登者需要額外的裝備，包括攀岩繩索、快扣（用來扣住保護點）、吊帶、頭盔與確保器。他們可能也會使用傳統攀岩裝備，例如固定式岩楔或彈簧岩楔，取決於攀登的類型。

• 抱石：抱石所需的裝備最少。攀登者通常會使用攀岩鞋、止滑粉來增強摩擦力，也會用防撞墊做墜落保護。一些抱石者可能也會用刷子清潔抓握點並提高摩擦力。

值得注意的是，雖然先鋒攀登通常在戶外的天然岩壁上進行，但也可以在室內的人工攀岩牆上練習。而抱石攀岩則既可以在戶外進行，也可以在室內進行，通常是在較矮的人工岩壁上或專門的抱石區域進行。

閱材透過 ChatGPT 的答覆，更正確地掌握了先鋒攀登與抱石之間的差異。他也決定依照每個重點逐一比較兩者的 Point-by-Point Method 來書寫這篇短文。

Step 3. 撰寫大綱

基於 ChatGPT 提供的資訊，閱材決定依照兩者的競賽方式（Game Format）、兩者所需的能力（Required Abilities）、兩者需要的設備與設施（Required Equipment and Facilities）等重點來比較先鋒攀登與抱石。這裡也請 ChatGPT 撰寫大綱看看。

Prompt

I am writing a 5 paragraph contrast essay that focuses on the three differences between the Lead and the Bouldering. I want you to write an essay outline. Body paragraphs contain the game format, required abilities, and required equipment and gym facility respectively.

我正在寫著重於先鋒攀登與抱石之間三種差異的五段式對照文。我要你撰寫一份文章的大綱。正文段落分別包括競賽方式、所需能力與需要的設備及體育館設施。

Sure! Here's an outline for your essay on the contrast between Lead Climbing and Bouldering:

I. Introduction

    A. Hook/Attention Grabber

    B. Brief explanation of Lead Climbing and Bouldering

C. Thesis statement: Lead Climbing and Bouldering differ in their game format, required abilities, and required equipment and gym facilities.

II. Body Paragraph 1: Game Format

   A. Explanation of Lead Climbing game format

      1. Climbing with a rope tied to the harness

      2. Following a predetermined route with anchors and quickdraws

      3. Clipping the rope into anchors for safety

      4. Goal: reaching the top with minimal falls or rests

   B. Explanation of Bouldering game format

      1. Climbing shorter, intense routes without ropes

      2. Tackling defined routes or sequences on a boulder or wall

      3. Emphasis on technique, power, and problem-solving abilities

      4. Goal: completing "problems" with precise movements and body coordination

III. Body Paragraph 2: Required Abilities

A. Required abilities in Lead Climbing

1. Endurance and stamina

2. Rope management skills and route reading abilities

3. Mental focus to handle potential falls

4. Rope-handling techniques, such as efficient clipping and slack management

B. Required abilities in Bouldering

1. Explosive power and agility

2. Strength for dynamic movements and sequences

3. Problem-solving skills and spatial awareness

4. Analysis of holds and body positioning for successful navigation

IV. Body Paragraph 3: Required Equipment and Gym Facility

A. Required equipment for Lead Climbing

1. Climbing harness, rope, quickdraws, carabiners, and helmet

2. Need for a climbing partner or belayer

3. Equipment for safety during falls

B. Required equipment for Bouldering

    1. Climbing shoes for improved grip

    2. Chalk for better hand friction

    3. Crash pads for safety during falls

C. Gym facility for Lead Climbing

    1. Taller walls with routes of varying difficulties

    2. Anchor placements for clipping the rope

    3. Facilities for lead climbing and belaying

D. Gym facility for Bouldering

    1. Shorter walls or dedicated Bouldering areas

    2. Challenging and dynamic boulder problems

    3. Design elements to test strength and technique

V. Conclusion

A. Restate thesis statement

B. Recap the main differences between Lead Climbing and Bouldering

C. Closing thoughts on the unique challenges and opportunities each style offers

D. Final statement highlighting the passion for

the sport and the joy of conquering challenging routes in both Lead Climbing and Bouldering.

當然！以下是你關於先鋒攀登與抱石之間對比的短文大綱：

I. 前言

　A. 引言／吸引注意

　B. 簡單說明先鋒攀登與抱石

　C. 主旨陳述句：先鋒攀登與抱石在競賽方式、所需能力與需要的設備及體育館設施等方面有所不同。

II. 正文第 1 段：競賽方式

　A. 先鋒攀登競賽方式說明

　　1. 用繫在吊帶上的繩索攀爬

　　2. 按照預先決定的路線，使用固定點與快扣進行攀登

　　3. 將繩索扣在固定點以確保安全

　　4. 目標：盡量避免墜落或休息而登頂

　B. 抱石競賽方式說明

　　1. 不用繩索，攀爬較短、強度較大的路線

　　2. 攻克巨石或岩牆上指定的路線或連續動作

3. 強調技術、力量與解決問題的能力

4. 目標：以精確的動作與身體協調解決「問
題」〔路線〕

III. 正文第 2 段：所需能力

　A. 先鋒攀登所需能力

　　1. 持久力與耐力

　　2. 繩索管理技能與路線判讀能力

　　3. 處理可能墜落的精神集中力

　　4. 繩索處理技巧，如有效率的掛繩與給繩
管理

　B. 抱石所需能力

　　1. 爆發力與靈活性

　　2. 動態動作與連續動作的力量

　　3. 解決問題的能力與空間意識

　　4. 分析抓握點與身體位置以完成攀登

IV. 正文第 3 段：所需設備與體育館設施

　A. 先鋒攀登所需設備

　　1. 攀岩吊帶、繩索、快扣、鉤環與頭盔

　　2. 需要一名攀岩夥伴（確保者）

　　3. 預防墜落的安全裝備

B. 抱石所需設備

    1. 提高抓地力的攀岩鞋

    2. 增強手部摩擦力的止滑粉

    3. 確保摔落時安全的防摔墊

C. 先鋒攀登的體育館設施

    1. 有多種難度路線的較高牆面

    2. 可將繩索扣上的錨栓

    3. 先鋒攀登與確保的設施

D. 抱石的體育館設施

    1. 較矮的牆面或專門的抱石區

    2. 具有挑戰性與動態的抱石路線

    3. 考驗力量與技術的設計元素

V. 結論

A. 重提主旨陳述句

B. 回顧先鋒攀登與抱石的主要差異

C. 對兩種方式各自的挑戰與機會總結想法

D. 結語，強調對這項運動的熱情，以及在先鋒
攀登與抱石運動中征服挑戰性路線的喜悅。

Step 4. 撰寫草稿

在前面的步驟，閔材透過 ChatGPT 的幫助，調查了關於先鋒攀登與抱石的資訊，並且產生了比較對照文所需的大綱。然後，閔材就參考大綱寫出了以下草稿。和其他類型的文章一樣，這個階段不允許使用 AI 工具。

Lead and Bouldering

(1st draft)

Have you ever tried climbing? If so, what kind of climbing did you do? As a sports, climbing is divided into 3 entries, Lead, Bouldering and Speed. Matches are played individually though ranking is sum of 3. Each event is quite characteristic and attractive. Speed has unique game method and seems far from others. But lead and Bouldering show some similarities and most of climbers combine two, so people are often confusing these. There are some differences between Lead and Bouldering.

First, Lead and Bouldering have different game format. Lead uses 15m artificial rock face. In the 6 minutes time limit, player who climbed the route higher gets higher score. If there are two more players who reached on the top, refree compares the time and determine the ranking. On the other hand, Bouldering is played on the 4~5m rock wall. Players don't wear harness because they do not climb high. There are some small route which has top and zone. Score is calculated based on the number of try and how many zone and top are touched.

Second, the two types of climbing require different ability. In the lead, players have only one chance. So level of each section is easy than Bouldering. Players do route finding carefully before climbing the wall. Muscular endurance, distribution of time and cautious conducting is important. In contrast, Bouldering has only time limit. Bouldering routes are more difficult and challenging. Players can solve problems their own creative way. Because of the gap in the physique, flexibilty and skills, Players choose variety ways. Power and dynamic moves determind rankings.

This entries need different kind of gym. To train lead, climbing center is required to pretty high ceiling. A large size gym or an outside climbing wall can provide this facility. In addition, Lead needs belayer who grip the rope. Gym has more equipment and more responsibility. If there is no climbing center like that around you, you can go classic climbing center and train muscular endurance by following long route. In spite of Lead, Bouldering use small space. The height is 4~5m and routes are short. You can easily find this type of gym in city.

Lead and Bouldering have its own game method, requiring ability and athletic facilities. I recommend both because they will help make your body different way. At the Paris Olympic, Lead and Bouldering are the detailed event of climbing and ranked together. So understanding similarities and differences between them become important.

先鋒攀登與抱石

（初稿）

你試過攀登運動嗎？如果有，是哪種攀登？作為體育競賽的攀登，分為三個項目：先鋒賽、抱石賽與速度賽。三種比賽分別進行，但依照三者的加總排名。每個項目都很有特色和吸引力。速度賽有其獨特的比賽方法，看起來和其他項目有很大的不同。但先鋒攀登與抱石有些相似之處，而大部分攀登者會將兩者結合起來，所以人們常常搞混這兩者。先鋒攀登與抱石有一些不同的地方。

　　首先，先鋒攀登與抱石的競賽方式不同。先鋒攀登使用 15 公尺高的人造岩牆。在 6 分鐘的時限內，攀爬路線越高的選手得分越高。如果還有兩名選手登頂，裁判會比較時間並決定名次。抱石則是在 4 至 5 公尺的岩牆上進行。因為攀爬高度不高，所以選手不會穿著安全吊帶。有一些有頂點和中點的小路線。分數依照嘗試的次數與觸及中點、頂點的次數計算。

　　其次，兩種攀爬方式需要不同的能力。在先鋒攀登中，選手只有一次機會。所以每一段的難度都比抱石簡單。選手在攀爬岩牆前會謹慎尋找路線。肌耐力、時間分配與謹慎進行很重要。相對地，抱石只有時間限制。抱石的路線比較難而有挑戰性。選手可以用自己的創意方式解決問題。由於體格、靈活性與技巧方面的差距，選手們選擇各種不同的方法。力量與動態動作決定排名。

　　這些比賽需要不一樣的體育場館。要訓練先鋒攀登，攀岩中心需要相當高的天花板。大型體育館或室外攀岩牆可以提供這種設施。此外，先鋒攀登也需要抓住繩子的確保者。體育館的設備較多，責任也較大。如果你附近沒有這樣的攀岩中心，可以去傳統的攀岩中心，透過攀登長距離的路線來訓練肌耐力。儘管有先鋒攀登，但抱石使用小空間。高度為 4 至 5 公尺，路線也短。在城市裡很容易找到這種類型的場館。

先鋒攀登與抱石有自己的競賽方式、所需能力與體育設施。我兩者都推薦，因為它們會幫助你的身體變得不同。在巴黎奧運會，先鋒攀登與抱石是攀登的細項比賽，並且合計排名。所以了解兩者之間的異同變得很重要。

Step 5. 修正與編輯

終於完成說明文的初稿了。從這個階段開始，閔材要參考同學與 ChatGPT 的回饋意見，用自己的語言修改文章。同學們覺得閔材的文章如何呢？他們看了閔材的文章後，雖然整體上給予高評價，但也指出許多不自然的表達方式與句子。此外，他們也建議強化結論部分。收到同學的這些回饋意見之後，閔材在 ChatGPT 輸入了以下五條提示詞來修改文章。他的文章產生了什麼變化呢？透過同學的回饋意見或 ChatGPT 修正的部分，同樣以顏色標示。

How about this article?

Is there any awkward sentence?

I think the ending of my essay is unclear. What should I put in the ending?

Could you briefly summarize it in one paragraph?

Are there any parts of my essay that are difficult to understand?

這篇文章怎麼樣？

有任何不自然的句子嗎？

我認為我的短文結尾不清楚。我應該在結尾加入什麼？

可以請你把它簡短總結成一段嗎？

我的短文有任何難以理解的部分嗎？

Lead and Bouldering

(2nd draft)

Have you ever tried climbing? If so, what kind of climbing did you do? As a sport, climbing is divided into 3 entries, Lead, Bouldering, and Speed. Matches are played individually though the ranking is a sum of 3. Each event is quite characteristic and attractive. Speed has a unique game method and seems far from others. But Lead and Bouldering show some similarities and most of the climbers combine two, so people are often confusing these. There are some differences between Lead and Bouldering.

First, Lead and Bouldering have different game formats. Lead uses a 15m artificial rock face. In the 6 minutes time limit, the player who climbed the route higher gets a higher score. If two or more players reach the top, the referee compares their times to determine the rankings. On the other hand, Bouldering is played on a 4~5m rock wall. Players don't wear harnesses because they do not climb high. Small routes have a Top and Zone. Top is a hold located at the end of route and Zone is a hold in the middle of the route. The score is calculated based on the number of tries and how many Zones and Tops are touched.

Second, the two types of climbing require different abilities. In the Lead, players have only one chance. Therefore, the level of each section is easier than Bouldering. Players do route finding carefully before climbing the wall. Muscular endurance, time management, and cautious conducting are important. In contrast, Bouldering has only a time limit, not a limited number of times. Bouldering routes are more difficult and challenging. Players can solve problems in their own creative way. Due to differences in physique, flexibility, and skills, players adapt their approaches. Power and dynamic moves determine rankings.

These entries need different kinds of gyms. To train Lead, the climbing center has to have a pretty high ceiling. A large size gym or an outside climbing wall can provide this facility. In addition, Lead needs a belayer who grips the rope. The gym has more equipment and more responsibility. If there is no climbing center like that around you, you can go to a classic climbing center and train muscular endurance by following long routes. Unlike Lead, Bouldering uses a small space. The height is 4~5m and routes are short. You can easily find this type of gym in a city.

Lead and Bouldering have their own game methods, required abilities and athletic facilities. So, whether you're a seasoned climber or a beginner, I encourage you to explore both disciplines and enjoy the immense satisfaction they bring. At the Paris Olympic in 2024, Lead and Bouldering are detailed events of climbing and ranking together. So understanding the similarities and differences between them become important.

先鋒攀登與抱石

（二稿）

你試過攀登運動嗎？如果有，是哪種攀登？作為體育競賽的攀登，分為三個項目：先鋒賽、抱石賽與速度賽。三種比賽分別進行，但依照三者的加總排名。每個項目都很有特色和吸引力。速度賽有其獨特的比賽方法，看起來和其他項目有很大的不同。但先鋒攀登與抱石有些相似之處，而大部分攀登者會將兩者結合起來，所以人們常常混淆兩者。先鋒攀登與抱石有一些不同的地方。

首先，先鋒攀登與抱石的競賽方式不同。先鋒攀登使用 15 公尺高的人造岩牆。在 6 分鐘的時限內，攀爬路線越高的選手得分越高。如果有兩名以上的選手登頂，裁判會比較他們的時間以決定名次。抱石則是在 4 至 5 公尺的岩牆上進行。因為攀爬高度不高，所以選手不會穿著安全吊帶。小的路線有頂點和中點。頂點是位於路線結尾的抓握點，中點是路線中途的抓握點。分數依照嘗試的次數與觸及中點、頂點的次數計算。

　　其次，兩種攀爬方式需要不同的能力。在先鋒攀登中，選手只有一次機會。所以每一段的難度都比抱石簡單。選手在攀爬岩牆前會謹慎尋找路線。肌耐力、時間管理與謹慎進行很重要。相對地，抱石只有時間限制，而沒有次數限制。抱石的路線比較難而有挑戰性。選手可以用自己的創意方式解決問題。由於體格、靈活性與技巧方面的差異，選手們會調整自己的方法。力量與動態動作決定排名。

　　這些比賽需要不一樣的體育場館。要訓練先鋒攀登，攀岩中心必須要有相當高的天花板。大型體育館或室外攀岩牆可以提供這種設施。此外，先鋒攀登也需要抓住繩子的確保者。體育館的設備較多，責任也較大。如果你附近沒有這樣的攀岩中心，可以去傳統的攀岩中心，透過攀登長距離的路線來訓練肌耐力。與先鋒攀登不同，抱石使用較小的空間。高度為 4 至 5 公尺，路線也短。在城市裡很容易找到這種類型的場館。

　　先鋒攀登與抱石有自己的競賽方式、所需能力與體育設施。所以，無論你是經驗豐富的攀岩者還是初學者，我都鼓勵你探索這兩種運動，享受它們帶來的無窮滿足。在 2024 年巴黎奧運會，先鋒攀登與抱石是攀登的細項比賽，並且合計排名。所以了解兩者之間的異同變得很重要。

在這個階段，必須用批判的眼光看待 ChatGPT 的修改事項。全盤接受 ChatGPT 的修改，不見得就會讓文章變好。如果覺得 ChatGPT 的修改不適合自己的文章，就不要接受。此外，即使句子經過修改而變得很好，知道原句中的什麼部分被改成怎樣還是很重要，因為明確了解其間的差異，是把句子寫得更好的第一步。在我們的英文寫作課，學生會用不同顏色標示接受 ChatGPT 或同學的回饋意見而修改的部分，並且在自我分析（Self-analysis）部分記錄改善了哪些地方。我們來看看閔材的自我分析寫了什麼。

Self-analysis

- I corrected the grammatical errors.
- Expressions that seemed like direct translations were naturally changed (distribution of time, require a high ceiling…)
- Added explanation of terms.

Here are the ChatGPT prompts I used.

- How about this article?
- Is there any awkward sentence?
- I think the ending of my essay is unclear. What should I put in the ending?

- Could you briefly summarize it in one paragraph?
- Are there any parts of my essay that are difficult to understand?

自我分析
－我修正了文法錯誤。
－看起來像直接翻譯的表達方式改得自然了（時間分配、需要高的天花板……）。
－添加了術語解釋。

以下是我使用的 ChatGPT 提示詞。
－這篇文章怎麼樣？
－有任何不自然的句子嗎？
－我認為我的短文結尾不清楚。我應該在結尾加入什麼？
－可以請你把它簡短總結成一段嗎？
－我的短文有任何難以理解的部分嗎？

此外，為了輕鬆找出自己一開始寫的初稿（第一份草稿）與接受同學與 ChatGPT 回饋後修改的版本（第二份草稿）之間的差異，閔材使用了下面的提示詞。

Make a table that compares the differences at the sentence level between the 1st draft and the 2nd draft.

請製作從句子層面比較初稿與二稿差異的表格。

Here is a table comparing the differences at the sentence level between the 1st draft and the 2nd draft:

1st Draft	2nd Draft
As a sports, climbing is divided into 3 entries	As a sport, climbing is divided into 3 entries
Matches are played individually though ranking is sum of 3	Matches are played individually though the ranking is a sum of 3
Speed has unique game method and seems far from others	Speed has a unique game method and seems far from others
But lead and Bouldering show some similarities and most of climbers combine two, so people are often confusing these	But lead and Bouldering show some similarities and most of the climbers combine two, so people are often confusing these
Lead uses 15m artificial rock face	Lead uses a 15m artificial rock face
If there are two more players who reached on the top, refree compares the time and determine the ranking	If two or more players reach the top, the referee compares their times to determine the rankings

On the other hand, Bouldering is played on the 4~5m rock wall	On the other hand, Bouldering is played on a 4~5m rock wall
Players don't wear harness because they do not climb high	Players don't wear harnesses because they do not climb high
There are some small route whice has top and zone	Small routes that have a Top and Zone
. . .	

　　這樣一來，初稿和二稿的差異就一目瞭然了吧？經由這個過程，學生可以掌握自己的句子是怎麼修改的。之後，閱材再次細讀二稿，並稍微修正各段落仍然不太自然的地方（以顏色標示的部分），寫出第三份草稿。

Paragraph 1 Speed has a unique game method and seems far from others.	Paragraph 1 Speed has a unique game method that sets it apart from the other two disciplines.

Paragraph 3 In contrast, Bouldering has only a time limit, not a limited number of times. Bouldering routes are more difficult and challenging. Players can solve problems in their own creative way. Due to differences in physique, flexibility, and skills, players adapt their approaches. Power and dynamic moves determine rankings.	Paragraph 3 In contrast, Bouldering is not limited by the number of attempts but instead has a time limit. Bouldering routes are more demanding and challenging. Due to differences in physique, flexibility, and skills, players solve problems in their own creative ways. Players use their momentary power, strong grip, and sense of balance. Power and dynamic moves determine rankings.
Paragraph 4 In addition, Lead needs a belayer who grips the rope. The gym has More equipment and more responsibility.	Paragraph 4 In addition, Lead needs a belayer who grips the rope. The gym requires additional equipment and has greater responsibility for accidents.
Paragraph 5 At the Paris olympic in 2024, Lead and Bouldering are detailed events of climbing and ranking together.	Paragraph 5 At the Paris Olympics in 2024, Lead and Bouldering are subcategories of climbing and ranking together.

Step 6. 撰寫最終版本

　　終於來到最後的階段。在這個階段，會對之前依照回饋意見修改的文章做最後確認並提交。對於說明文，務必特別注意以下事項。

- 明確的結構

　　文章必須具有明確且統一的結構。文章應該由前言、正文、結論構成，而每一段都要有明確的主題句，以及支持主題句的主張、例子與證據。

- 邏輯連貫性

　　文章裡的想法與主張應該以有邏輯的順序推進。段落間應該維持邏輯上的關聯，每個句子與段落也應該自然地衔接。

- 具體例子與證據

　　應該提供支持主張的具體例子與證據。引用歷史事件、研究結果、專家意見等等，有助於強化主張。

- 客觀與中立性

　　文章應該盡可能客觀、中立。支持主張的資訊或證據應該出自可信的出處。

- 風格與文法

　　寫作時應該使用適當的風格與文法。確認句子結構與拼字，以及風格是否適當且適合目標讀者，是很重要的。

- 徹底檢查

　　最後寫好的文章應該徹底檢查。必須找出錯字、文法錯誤與邏輯不一致的地方並加以修正，以及在情境中是否能讓人理解。

- 流暢的轉承

　　每個段落、句子之間，應該有自然的轉承。寫作時最好強調段落間的邏輯連結，並使用轉承句或轉折詞，使讀者能清楚看出文章內容的推進。

- 一致性

　　風格、引用形式、表達方式等等，應該維持一致性。一致性能為閱讀文章的讀者帶來穩定感。

　　此外，最後也應該再次檢查錯字、文法、邏輯、表達方式等，並思考是否有更好的表達方式。閔材使用 Grammarly 程式，在程式建議的各種修改事項中，對包括標點符號與重複單字在內的七個地方進行修改。現在，詳細比較先鋒攀登與抱石的說明文終於完成了。請跟草稿比較一下，看看文章有什麼不同。

Lead and Bouldering

(final)

Have you ever tried climbing? If so, what kind of climbing did you do? As a sport, climbing is divided into three entries, Lead, Bouldering, and Speed. Matches are played individually though the ranking is a sum of 3. Each event is quite characteristic and attractive. Speed has a unique game method that sets it apart from the other two disciplines. But Lead and Bouldering show some similarities and most climbers combine the two, so people often confuse these. There are some differences between Lead and Bouldering.

First, Lead and Bouldering have different game formats. Lead uses a 15m artificial rock face. In the 6 minutes time limit, the player who climbed the route higher gets a higher score. If two or more players reach the top, the referee compares their times to determine the rankings. On the other hand, Bouldering is played on a 4~5m rock wall. Players don't wear harnesses because they do not climb high. Small routes have a Top and Zone. The top is a hold located at the end of the route, and Zone is a hold in the middle of the route. The score is calculated based on the number of tries and how many Zones and Tops are touched.

Second, the two types of climbing require different abilities. In the Lead, players have only one chance. Therefore, the level of each section is easier than Bouldering. Players do route finding carefully before climbing the wall. Muscular endurance, time management, and cautious conduct are important. In contrast, Bouldering is not limited by the number of attempts but instead has a time limit. Bouldering routes are more demanding and challenging. Due to differences in physique, flexibility, and skills, players solve problems in their own creative ways. Players use their momentary power, strong grip, and sense of balance. Power and dynamic moves determine rankings.

These entries need different kinds of gyms. To train leaders, the climbing center has to have a high ceiling. A large size gym or an outside climbing wall can provide this facility. In addition, Lead needs a belayer who grips the rope. The gym requires additional equipment and has greater responsibility for accidents. If there is no climbing center like that around you, you can go to a classic climbing center and train muscular endurance by following long routes. Unlike Lead, Bouldering uses a small space. The height is 4~5m, and the routes are short. But you can easily find a steep wall in the gyms. In these gyms, mats are used for safety. To make various problems, the gym uses unique holds and creates new problems periodically. You can easily find this type of gym in a city.

Lead and Bouldering have their own game methods, required abilities and athletic facilities. So, whether you're a seasoned climber or a beginner, I encourage you to explore both disciplines and enjoy the immense satisfaction they bring. At the Paris Olympics in 2024, Lead and Bouldering are subcategories of climbing and ranking together. So understanding the similarities and differences between them becomes essential.

先鋒攀登與抱石

（最終版）

你試過攀登運動嗎？如果有，是哪種攀登？作為體育競賽的攀登，分為三個項目：先鋒賽、抱石賽與速度賽。三種比賽分別進行，但依照三者的加總排名。每個項目都很有特色和吸引力。速度賽有其獨特的比賽方法，使它和其他兩項有所差異。但先鋒攀登與抱石有些相似之處，而大部分攀登者會將兩者結合起來，所以人們常常混淆兩者。先鋒攀登與抱石有一些不同的地方。

首先，先鋒攀登與抱石的競賽方式不同。先鋒攀登使用 15 公尺高的人造岩牆。在 6 分鐘的時限內，攀爬路線越高的選手得分越高。如果有兩名以上的選手登頂，裁判會比較他們的時間以決定名次。抱石則是在 4 至 5 公尺的岩牆上進行。因為攀爬高度不高，所以選手不會穿著安全吊帶。小的路線有頂點和中點。頂點是位於路線結尾的抓握點，中點是路線中途的抓握點。分數依照嘗試的次數與觸及中點、頂點的次數計算。

其次，兩種攀爬方式需要不同的能力。在先鋒攀登中，選手只有一次機會。所以，每一段的難度都比抱石簡單。選手在攀爬岩牆前會謹慎尋找路線。肌耐力、時間管理與謹慎進行很重要。相對地，抱石不限制嘗試次數，而是限制時間。抱石的路線比較困難而有挑戰性。由於體格、靈活性與技巧方面的差異，選手會以自己的創意方式解決問題。選手會利用自己的瞬間爆發力、強大的握力與平衡感。力量與動態動作決定排名。

這些比賽需要不一樣的體育場館。要訓練先鋒攀登者，攀岩中心必須要有很高的天花板。大型體育館或室外攀岩牆可以提供這種設施。此外，先鋒攀登也需要抓住繩子的確保者。體育館需要額外的設備，對事故也負有更大的責任。如果你附近沒有這樣的攀岩中心，可以去傳統的攀岩中心，透過攀登長距離的路線來訓練肌耐力。與先鋒攀登不同，抱石使用較小的空間。高度為 4 至 5 公尺，路線也短。但在抱石館很容易就能找到陡峭的牆面。在這些場館裡，會使用墊子確保安全。為了創造各種路線（problem），場館使用獨特的抓握點並定期創造新的路線。在城市裡很容易找到這種類型的場館。

先鋒攀登與抱石有自己的競賽方式、所需能力與體育設施。所以，無論你是經驗豐富的攀岩者還是初學者，我都鼓勵你探索這兩種運動，享受它們帶來的無窮滿足。在 2024 年的巴黎奧運會，先鋒攀登與抱石是攀登的子項目，並且合計排名。所以了解兩者之間的異同變得至關重要。

論說文（Argumentative Essay）：載煜的寫作

最後要看的是載煜撰寫論說文的每個階段。

Step 1. 選定主題

論說文，或者稱為說服性文章，是關於特定主題兩種相反意見的寫作類型。這種文章在學校主要當成論述的作業，文章的目的是有邏輯地展現令人信服的主張，藉此說服讀者。

Recommend good topics for an argumentative essay.

請推薦適合寫成論說文的主題。

Certainly! Here are some possible topic ideas for an argumentative essay:

1. The Effects of Social Media on Mental Health: Argue that social media use can have negative effects on mental health, and discuss potential solutions for mitigating these effects.

2. The Ethics of Genetic Engineering: Argue for or against the use of genetic engineering in humans or animals, and discuss the potential benefits and drawbacks of this technology.

3. The Pros and Cons of School Uniforms: Argue for or against the use of school uniforms, and discuss the potential benefits and drawbacks of this policy.

4. The Impact of Video Games on Violence: Argue for or against the idea that violent video games

contribute to real-world violence, and discuss potential solutions for addressing this issue.

5. The Benefits and Drawbacks of Online Learning: Argue for or against the use of online learning in education, and discuss the potential benefits and drawbacks of this approach.

6. The Ethics of Animal Rights: Argue for or against the idea that animals have rights, and discuss potential solutions for protecting animal welfare.

7. The Impact of Climate Change on Human Populations: Argue that climate change is a significant threat to human populations, and discuss potential solutions for mitigating its effects.

8. The Ethics of Capital Punishment: Argue for or against the use of capital punishment, and discuss potential alternatives and solutions for addressing crime.

I hope these ideas help you with your argumentative essay!

當然！以下是一些論說文可能的主題構想：

1. 社交媒體對心理健康的影響：論證社交媒體的使用可能對心理健康產生負面影響，並討論減輕這些影響的可能解決方法。

2. 基因工程的倫理：支持或反對在人類或動物身上使用基因工程，並討論這種技術可能的好處與壞處。

3. 學校制服的利弊：支持或反對使用學校制服，並討論這個政策可能的利弊。

4. 電玩遊戲對暴力的影響：支持或反對暴力電玩遊戲助長現實世界暴力的觀點，並討論這個問題可能的解決方法。

5. 線上學習的利弊：支持或反對在教育中使用線上學習，並討論這種方法可能的好處與壞處。

6. 動物權利的倫理：支持或反對動物享有權利的觀點，並討論保護動物福利的可能解決方案。

7. 氣候變遷對人類的影響：論證氣候變遷對人類是重大的威脅，並討論減輕氣候變遷影響的可能解決方案。

8. 死刑的倫理：支持或反對使用死刑，並討論處理犯罪問題的可能替代方案與解決方案。

希望這些構想對您的論說文有幫助！

在 ChatGPT 建議的各種主題中，載煜選擇了「線上學習的利弊」（5. The Benefits and Drawbacks of Online Learning），因為他在 COVID-19 疫情期間曾經長期接受遠距教學，而對線上學習有許多想法。載煜想站在反對線上學習的立場，寫一篇文章來說服贊成線上學習的人。決定主題之後，就接著看看思考構想的階段吧。

Step 2. 思考構想

論說文的內容包括自己的主張，以及支持這個主張的客觀證據。在文中會討論和自己的主張相反的意見並加以反駁，同時更加強調自己的邏輯。論說文的目的，是以有邏輯的結構與論證說服讀者，所以必須對主題進行徹底的調查。載煜在寫文章之前，請 ChatGPT 幫忙自己掌握線上學習的優缺點。此外，也調查了相對於贊成線上學習者的反面論點（Counter-Argument）並提出反駁（Refutation）。

Do some research on the pros and cons of online learning.

研究一下線上學習的優缺點。

Certainly! Here are some pros and cons of online learning:

• Pros of Online Learning:

- Flexibility: Online learning provides the flexibility to access course materials and lectures at any time and from any location with an internet connection. This flexibility allows students to balance their education with work, family, or other commitments.

- Accessibility: Online learning eliminates geographical barriers, allowing students to access education regardless of their location. It provides opportunities for individuals who may not have access to traditional educational institutions, such as those in remote areas or with physical limitations.

- Diverse Learning Options: Online platforms offer a wide range of courses and programs, allowing students to choose from various subjects and disciplines. This enables learners to pursue their specific interests and passions, or gain specialized knowledge in niche areas.

- Self-Paced Learning: Online courses often offer self-paced learning options, allowing students to progress through the material at their own speed. This accommodates different learning styles and preferences, providing a personalized learning experience.

- Cost-Effectiveness: Online learning can be more cost-effective compared to traditional education. It eliminates expenses associated with commuting, accommodation, and sometimes textbooks. Additionally, online courses often have lower tuition fees, making education more affordable.

• Cons of Online Learning:

- Limited Social Interaction: Online learning reduces face-to-face interaction with peers and instructors, which can hinder social development, collaboration, and networking opportunities. It may lack the vibrant learning environment and social dynamics found in traditional classrooms.

- Lack of Hands-on Experience: Some subjects, such as certain laboratory-based or practical courses, may be challenging to replicate effectively in an online setting. Hands-on experiences and physical interaction with equipment or materials may be limited.

- Need for Self-Motivation and Discipline: Online learning requires self-motivation and discipline as students are responsible for managing their time, staying on track with assignments, and overcoming distractions. This level of self-direction may not suit all learners and can lead to procrastination or a lack of accountability.

- Technical Challenges: Online learning relies heavily on technology, and technical difficulties or lack of access to reliable internet can hinder the learning experience. Technical issues can be frustrating and disrupt the flow of learning, requiring troubleshooting and potential delays.

- Limited Personalized Support: Online learning may offer limited opportunities for immediate and personalized support. Students may face challenges in receiving timely feedback, clarifying doubts, or engaging in real-time discussions with instructors and peers.

It's important to note that the effectiveness and suitability of online learning can vary based on individual learning styles, preferences, and the quality of the online program or institution. Online learning can be a valuable educational option, especially when combined with appropriate support mechanisms and resources to address the potential limitations.

當然！以下是線上學習的一些優點與缺點：

‧線上學習的優點：

－彈性：線上學習提供在任何時間、任何地點透過網路連線取得課程材料與聽課的彈性。這種彈性使學生在受教育之餘可以兼顧工作、家庭或其他事務。

－易取得性：線上學習消除了地理障礙，使學生無論身處何地都能接受教育。它為可能無法前往傳統教育機構的人，例如偏遠地區或有身體方面限制的人，提供受教育的機會。

－多樣化的學習選擇：線上平台提供廣泛的課程與學程，讓學生能選擇不同的科目與學科。這使學習者能夠追求自己的特定興趣與愛好，或者獲得小眾領域的專業知識。

－自定進度學習：線上課程通常提供自定進度的學習選項，允許學生以自己的速度學習材料。這適應了不同的學習風格與偏好，提供個人化的學習體驗。

－成本效益：與傳統教育相比，線上學習可能更具成本效益。它省去了通勤、住宿，有時還省去了教科書方面的費用。此外，線上課程的學費通常較低，使教育更加經濟實惠。

・線上學習的缺點：

－社交互動有限：線上學習減少了與同儕及教師的面對面互動，這可能會阻礙社交發展、合作以及建立人際關係的機會。它可能缺乏傳統課堂中充滿活力的學習環境與社會動力。

－缺乏實務經驗：有些科目，例如某些以實驗室為基礎或實踐的課程，可能很難在網路環境中有效複製。實務經驗以及與設備或材料的實際互動可能會受到限制。

－需要自我激勵與紀律：線上學習需要自我激勵與紀律，因為學生有責任管理自己的時間、按時完成作業並克服分心。這種程度的自我引導可能不適合所有學習者，而且可能導致拖延或缺乏責任感。

－技術挑戰：線上學習非常依賴技術，而技術上的困難或無法連上可靠的網路，可能阻礙學習體驗。技術問題可能令人沮喪、擾亂學習進行，需要排除故障並可能造成延誤。

－有限的個人化支持：線上學習提供即時且個人化支援的機會可能有限。學生有可能很難獲得及時回饋、釐清疑惑或與教師及同儕進行即時討論。

值得注意的是，線上學習的有效性與合適性可能因為個人學習風格、偏好以及線上學程或機構的品質而有所不同。線上學習可以是有價值的教育選擇，尤其是在結合適當的支持機制與資源來解決潛在限制的情況下。

👤 Do some research on the logic to rebut pros.

研究一下反駁贊成意見的邏輯。

⑤ Certainly! Here are some counterarguments to the pros of online learning:

- Flexibility: While online learning offers flexibility, the lack of a set schedule and physical classroom environment can lead to challenges in time management and maintaining discipline. In-person classes provide structure and regular interaction with instructors, which can enhance accountability and engagement.

- Accessibility: While online learning addresses accessibility barriers, it can create new barriers for individuals who lack access to reliable internet or necessary technology. This can further marginalize disadvantaged communities and limit their educational opportunities. In-person education ensures equal access for all students, regardless of their technological resources.

- Diverse Learning Options: While online platforms provide diverse course options, the quality and credibility of these courses can vary significantly. Not all online courses are created equal, and there may be a lack of regulation and oversight in the online education space. Traditional educational institutions often have established reputations and accreditation processes, ensuring a certain level of quality and rigor in the curriculum.

- Self-Paced Learning: While self-paced learning can benefit some students, it may not be suitable for everyone. Some students thrive in structured learning environments with clear deadlines and regular interaction with instructors and peers. Without the external accountability and structure of traditional classrooms, self-paced online courses can lead to procrastination, lack of motivation, and a shallow understanding of the subject matter.

- Cost-Effectiveness: While online learning can reduce certain costs, it may not always provide the same value as traditional education. In-person education often offers opportunities for hands-on experiences, networking, internships, and access to specialized resources like libraries and laboratories. These experiences may not be adequately replicated in an online setting, limiting the overall educational experience.

It's important to approach online learning with a critical mindset, considering both the benefits and potential drawbacks. A balanced approach that combines online and traditional educational methods may provide the most comprehensive and effective learning experience.

當然！以下是對於線上學習優點的反面論點：

－彈性：雖然線上學習提供彈性，但由於沒有固定的時間表和實際的教室環境，可能會在時間管理和維持紀律方面帶來挑戰。面對面課程則提供結構與和教師的定期互動，可以增強責任感和參與度。

－易取得性：雖然線上學習解決了易取得性的障礙，但對於無法連上可靠的網路或使用必要技術的人而言，線上學習可能會造成新的障礙。這可能進一步邊緣化弱勢群體，限制他們受教育的機會。面對面教育可確保所有學生，無論其技術資源如何，都能平等地接受教育。

－多樣化的學習選擇：雖然線上平台提供多樣化的課程選擇，但這些課程的品質和可信度可能有很大的差異。並非所有線上課程都有相同的水準，而且線上教育領域可能缺乏監管與監督。傳統教育機構通常有已經確立的聲譽與認證過程，可確保課程具有一定的品質和嚴謹性。

－自定進度學習：雖然自定進度學習能讓一些學生受益，但可能不適合所有人。有些學生在有明確的截止期限、與教師和同儕定期互動的結構化學習環境成效良好。沒有傳統課堂的外部責任與結構，自定進度的線上課程可能會導致拖延、缺乏動力以及對主題的淺薄理解。

－成本效益：雖然線上學習可以降低一定的成本，但它提供的價值並不一定與傳統教育相同。面對面教育往往提供實務經驗、人際關係建立、實習以及使用圖書館和實驗室等專用資源的機會。這些體驗可能無法在線上環境充分複製，從而限制整體教育體驗。

重要的是，要以批判的心態看待線上學習，既要考慮到好處，也要考慮到潛在的缺點。結合線上和傳統教育方法的平衡方式可能會提供最全面、最有效的學習體驗。

從上面的內容可以看到，ChatGPT 用來收集特定主題的各種相關想法，是很好的工具。但如果是統計或研究資料的話，必須再次確認收集來的資料的正確性，因為 ChatGPT 常常把子虛烏有的事說得像真的一樣，或者給予錯誤的資訊。請親自查看刊載統計或研究資料的網站，確認是否真的有這樣的研究，以及其中的主要事項。

Step 3. 撰寫大綱

論說文是藉由合理的主張與適當的證據說服讀者的文體。一般而言，會在文章開頭的前言段落提及問題，並提出核心主張。在正文部分，會以客觀證據與主張進行論證，而最後的結論段落則重新強調主張，同時提出替代方案與解決方法。載煜請 ChatGPT 寫出說服贊成線上學習的人轉向相反立場的文章大綱。

I'm writing a persuasive essay against online learning to convince people who favor it. I need you to create an efficient outline for my essay. The first three body paragraphs will show cons of online learning with examples and the last body paragraph should include a counterargument and rebuttals.

我正在寫反對線上學習的論説文來説服贊成的人。我要你為我的文章寫出一份有效率的大綱。前三個正文段落將呈現線上學習的缺點並附上例子，而正文的最後一段要包含反面論點與反駁。

Certainly! Here's an efficient outline for your persuasive essay against online learning:

I. Introduction

A. Hook or attention-grabbing statement to engage the reader

B. Background information on online learning and its increasing popularity

C. Clear thesis statement expressing your opposition to online learning

II. Body Paragraph 1: Lack of Personal Interaction and Social Development

    A. Explanation of the limitations of online platforms in facilitating face-to-face interaction

    B. Discussion on the importance of in-person communication and socialization for students

    C. Examples or evidence showcasing the negative consequences of reduced personal interaction and limited social development in online learning

III. Body Paragraph 2: Reduced Teacher-Student Engagement and Support

    A. Explanation of the challenges in establishing meaningful connections in online classrooms

    B. Discussion on the importance of personalized feedback and guidance for effective learning

    C. Examples or evidence highlighting the negative effects of reduced teacher-student engagement and support in online learning

IV. Body Paragraph 3: Distractions and Lack of Focus

A. Discussion on potential distractions and reduced focus in non-traditional learning environments

B. Explanation of how distractions can hinder academic performance and hinder learning outcomes

C. Examples or evidence demonstrating the negative consequences of distractions in online learning

V. Body Paragraph 4: Counterargument and Rebuttals

A. Present a counterargument in favor of online learning (e.g., flexibility, access to resources)

B. Refute the counterargument by providing evidence and reasoning against it

C. Address the limitations and potential drawbacks of the counterargument to strengthen your position

VI. Conclusion

A. Restatement of the thesis statement

emphasizing your opposition to online learning

B. Summary of the key points discussed in the essay, including the cons of online learning

C. Call to action, encouraging readers to reconsider their support for online learning

D. Closing statement that leaves a lasting impression on the reader

Remember to provide strong evidence, examples, and persuasive language in the body paragraphs to support your arguments effectively. In the counterargument section, anticipate potential counterarguments and address them with logical reasoning and evidence to strengthen your position. Good luck with your essay!

當然！以下是你反對線上學習的論說文的高效率大綱：

I. 前言
  A. 引言或吸引讀者注意力的敘述
  B. 關於線上學習及其日益普及的背景資訊

C.清楚的主旨陳述句，表達你對線上學習的反對意見

II. 正文第 1 段：缺乏人際互動與社會發展

A. 說明網路平台在促進面對面互動方面的侷限

B. 討論面對面溝通與社交對學生的重要性

C. 顯示線上學習減少人際互動並限制社會發展帶來的負面影響舉例或證據

III. 正文第 2 段：師生參與和支援減少

A. 說明在網路課堂中建立有意義的連結所面臨的挑戰

B. 討論個人化回饋與指導對有效學習的重要性

C. 強調線上學習中師生參與和支持減少帶來負面影響的例子或證據

IV.正文第 3 段：分心因素與注意力不集中

A. 討論非傳統學習環境中潛在的分心因素與注意力降低的問題

B. 說明分心如何妨礙學業表現與學習效果

C. 呈現線上學習時分心因素造成負面影響的例子或證據

V. 正文第 4 段：反面論點與反駁

   A. 提出支持線上學習的反面論點（例如彈性、資源的取得）

   B. 藉由提供相反的證據與推理來反駁反面論點

   C. 處理反面論點的侷限與可能的缺點，加強自己的立場

VI. 結論

   A. 重提主旨陳述句，強調自己反對線上學習

   B. 總結文章中討論的要點，包括線上學習的缺點

   C. 行動呼籲，鼓勵讀者重新考慮對線上學習的支持

   D. 讓讀者留下持久印象的結語

　　切記在正文段落提供有力的證據、例子和有說服力的語言，以有效支持你的論點。在反面論點部分，預測可能出現的反面論點，並且用邏輯推理與證據加以解決，加強您的立場。祝您寫作順利！

　　在 ChatGPT 的幫助下，完成了既有邏輯又有說服力的大綱。載煜檢視大綱之後，決定在正文第二段增加線上學習導致缺乏實務經驗（lack of hands-on experience）的內

容。有時候 ChatGPT 產出的大綱不太令人滿意，這時可以自己動手修改，或者在提示詞中更具體地表明大綱要包含的內容，就可以看到更好的大綱。

Step 4. 撰寫草稿

在這個階段，載煜以修改過的大綱為基礎，自己寫好了這篇論說文的草稿。

The Limitation of Online Education

(1st draft)

Online education has rapidly gained popularity in recent years by its convenience and as an alternative to traditional education. Since the COVID-19 pandemic, we had to get ourselves in our own houses, seeing friends online. However, while online education offers a big advantage, I disagree that online education is the best choice for all students. In this essay, I would like to reveal the drawbacks of online education and highlight the aspects that fall short compared to traditional education.

One of the major drawbacks of online education is

limited personal interaction. In a traditional classroom setting, students can have face-to-face discussions, ask questions in real-time, and receive immediate feedback from their teachers. These interpersonal interactions make deeper understanding and foster communication and collaboration among students. In contrast, online education relies heavily on digital communication platforms, which can be impersonal. The absence of real-time interaction can hinder student engagement, making it challenging for learners to establish connections.

Another disadvantage of online education is that we can't experience hands-on learning experiences. Physical presence and active participation are crucial for comprehensive comprehension in many subjects, such as laboratory-based sciences or performing arts. Practical experimentation, group activities, and live demonstrations are very important in effective learning. Unfortunately, online education platforms often struggle to replicate such hands-on experiences. Students may miss out on the chance to develop essential skills through direct practice and experimentation, limiting their overall educational growth.

Finally, online education fails to promote active student participation in the same way as traditional classroom settings. In a physical classroom, students are more likely to focus on the lesson, and participate in discussions, debates, and group activities. The presence of instructors creates a dynamic learning environment that encourages students to contribute their ideas, share diverse perspectives, and develop critical thinking skills. In contrast, online education platforms may lack the immediacy that face-to-face interactions bring. Also, the absence of instructors makes students feel that they are not being watched and the instructors won't know that they aren't participating in the lesson. These days, access to the internet is so easy and this makes students to not pay attention to the lesson and play games or watch youtube during class.

Proponents of online education often highlight its flexibility and accessibility as major advantages. They argue that online learning allows individuals to study at their own pace, from any location. While these aspects may be beneficial for certain individuals, it is essential to recognize that not all learners thrive in independent, self-paced environments. Some students may require the structure and guidance provided by traditional classrooms to maintain motivation and discipline. Additionally, accessibility to online education can be limited by factors such as the digital divide, where individuals with limited internet access or technology resources are at a disadvantage.

In conclusion, the limitations of online education, including the lack of personal interaction, reduced hands-on learning opportunities, and failure to make students participate actively, make education worth less than the original. As we move forward, it is inevitable to strike a balance between the advantages of online education and the unique benefits of traditional classrooms, ensuring that learners have access to the most effective and comprehensive learning environments.

線上教育的侷限

（初稿）

近年來，線上教育藉著它的便利性，以及作為替代傳統教育的方式而迅速普及。自從 COVID-19 大流行以來，我們不得不待在家裡，在網路上見朋友。然而，雖然線上教育提供很大的優勢，但我不同意線上教育是所有學生的最佳選擇。在這篇文章中，我想揭示線上教育的缺點，並強調與傳統教育相比不足的方面。

線上教育的主要缺點之一是人際互動有限。在傳統課堂環境中，學生可以面對面討論、即時發問，並且立即得到老師的回饋。這些人際互動會加深理解，並促進學生之間的溝通與合作。相對地，線上教育非常依賴數位溝通平台，而這可能是沒有人情味的。缺乏即時互動可能阻礙學生的參與，使學習者難以建立聯繫。

線上教育的另一個缺點是我們無法體驗實務上的學習經驗。在許多科目中，身臨其境和積極參與對於全面的理解至關重要，例如以實驗室為基礎的科學或表演藝術。實際實驗、小組活動與現場示範對於有效學習非常重要。遺憾的是，線上教育平台往往難以複製這種實務經驗。學生可能會錯過藉由直接實踐與實驗發展必要技能的機會，從而限制他們的整體教育成長。

最後，線上教育無法像傳統課堂環境一般促進學生積極參與。在實體課堂上，學生比較有可能專心聽課，並且參與討論、辯論和小組活動。教師的在場創造出動態的學習環境，鼓勵學生貢獻自己的想法、分享不同的觀點，並且培養批判思考能力。相對地，線上教育平台可能缺乏面對面互動所帶來的即時性。此外，教師不在場會使學生覺得沒有受到監視、教師不會知道他們沒有參與課程。在這個時代，上網很容易，使得學生上課時不專心聽課，而且會玩遊戲或看 youtube。

　　線上教育的支持者常常強調它的彈性與易取得性，視為主要的優勢。他們主張，線上學習讓個人能在任何地點按照自己的步調學習。雖然這些方面可能對某些人有益，但我們必須認知到，並非所有學習者都能在獨立、自定進度的環境表現良好。有些學生可能需要傳統課堂提供的結構與指導來保持學習動力和紀律。此外，線上教育的可取得性可能會受到數位落差之類因素的限制，這指的是只能取得有限的網路連線或科技資源的人處於弱勢地位。

　　總之，線上教育的侷限，包括缺乏人際互動、減少實務學習機會，以及無法使學生積極參與，使得教育的價值比原本來得低。在進步的過程中，我們必須在線上教育的優勢與傳統課堂獨有的益處之間取得平衡，確保學習者得到最有效、最全面的學習環境。

Step 5. 修正與編輯

　　在這個階段，要請同儕和 AI 工具針對草稿給予回饋意見。如同之前說過的，我們的英文寫作課會用微軟 Teams 應用程式的共用檔案功能，對同學的文章提供回饋意見。

載煜從同學那邊得到了什麼意見呢？

　　在各種回饋中，載煜最注重的建議，是希望他提出更詳細的證據來支持自己的主張。載煜認為，為了強化證明主張的證據，應該提到比較具體的研究或例子，所以他使用了下面的提示詞。他從 ChatGPT 的回答中選擇了比較好的部分，並且使用在初稿上，而寫出了二稿。

Prompt

👤 Make the following essay more persuasive by materializing the evidence.

請將證據具體化，使以下短文更有說服力。

The Limitation of Online Education

(2nd draft)

Online education has rapidly gained popularity in recent years by its convenience and as an alternative to traditional education. Since the COVID-19 pandemic, we had to get ourselves in our own houses, seeing friends online. However, while online education offers a big advantage, I disagree that online education is the best choice for all students. In this essay, I would like to reveal the drawbacks of online education and highlight the aspects that fall short compared to traditional education.

One of the major drawbacks of online education is limited personal interaction. In a traditional classroom setting, students can have face-to-face discussions, ask questions in real-time, and receive immediate feedback from their teachers. A study conducted by the National Education Association found that in-person interactions fostered deeper understanding and improved communication and collaboration among students. In contrast, online education relies heavily on digital communication platforms, which can be impersonal. According to a survey by EdSurge, 72% of online learners reported feeling isolated and disconnected due to the lack of real-time interaction. The absence of real-time interaction can hinder student engagement, making it challenging for learners to establish connections.

Another disadvantage of online education is the inability to experience hands-on learning. Physical presence and active participation are crucial for comprehension in many subjects, such as laboratory-based sciences or performing arts. Practical experimentation, group activities, and live demonstrations are very important in effective learning. Unfortunately, online education platforms often struggle to replicate such hands-on experiences. Visualize students watching pre-recorded videos of experiments or simulations, missing out on the opportunity to actively participate and engage with the material. This limitation restricts students' ability to fully grasp complex concepts and apply them in real-world scenarios.

Finally, online education fails to promote active student participation in the same way as traditional classroom settings. In a physical classroom, students are more likely to focus on the lesson, and participate in discussions, debates, and group activities. A report by the U.S. Department of Education found that active student engagement enhances critical thinking skills and promotes knowledge retention. The presence of instructors creates a dynamic learning environment that encourages students to contribute their ideas, share diverse perspectives, and develop critical thinking skills.

In contrast, online education platforms may lack the immediacy that face-to-face interactions bring. Also, the absence of instructors makes students feel that they are not being watched and the instructors won't know that they aren't participating in the lesson. These days, access to the internet is so easy and this makes students to not pay attention to the lesson and play games or watch youtube during class.

Proponents of online education often highlight its flexibility and accessibility as major advantages. They argue that online learning allows individuals to study at their own pace, from any location. While these aspects may be beneficial for certain individuals, it is essential to recognize that not all learners thrive in independent, self-paced environments. Some students require the structure and guidance provided by traditional classrooms to maintain motivation and discipline. Additionally, accessibility to online education can be limited by factors such as the digital divide, where individuals with limited internet access or technology resources are at a disadvantage.

In conclusion, the limitations of online education, including the lack of personal interaction, reduced hands-on learning opportunities, and failure to make students participate actively, make education worth less than traditional education. As we move forward, it is inevitable to strike a balance between the advantages of online education and the unique benefits of traditional classrooms, ensuring that learners have access to the most effective and comprehensive learning environments.

線上教育的侷限

（二稿）

　　近年來，線上教育藉著它的便利性，以及作為替代傳統教育的方式而迅速普及。自從 COVID-19 大流行以來，我們不得不待在家裡，在網路上見朋友。然而，雖然線上教育提供很大的優勢，但我不同意線上教育是所有學生的最佳選擇。在這篇文章中，我想揭示線上教育的缺點，並強調與傳統教育相比不足的方面。

　　線上教育的主要缺點之一是人際互動有限。在傳統課堂環境中，學生可以面對面討論、即時發問，並且立即得到老師的回饋。美國國家教育協會進行的一項研究發現，面對面的互動加深了理解，並且改善了學生之間的溝通與合作。相對地，線上教育非常依賴數位溝通平台，而這可能是沒有人情味的。根據 EdSurge 的調查，72% 的線上學習者表示，由於缺乏即時互動，他們感到孤獨並缺乏連結。缺乏即時互動可能阻礙學生的參與，使學習者難以建立聯繫。

線上教育的另一個缺點是無法體驗實務學習。在許多科目中，身臨其境和積極參與對於理解至關重要，例如以實驗室為基礎的科學或表演藝術。實際實驗、小組活動與現場示範對於有效學習非常重要。遺憾的是，線上教育平台往往難以複製這種實務經驗。想像一下，學生在觀看預先錄製的實驗或模擬影片時，失去了積極參與及接觸材料的機會。這種侷限性限制了學生充分掌握複雜概念並應用於真實世界情況的能力。

最後，線上教育無法像傳統課堂環境一般促進學生積極參與。在實體課堂上，學生比較有可能專心聽課，並且參與討論、辯論和小組活動。美國教育部的一份報告發現，學生積極參與會提高批判性思考能力，並且促進知識的保持。教師的在場創造出動態的學習環境，鼓勵學生貢獻自己的想法、分享不同的觀點，並且培養批判思考能力。相對地，線上教育平台可能缺乏面對面互動所帶來的即時性。此外，教師不在場會使學生覺得沒有受到監視、教師不會知道他們沒有參與課程。在這個時代，上網很容易，使得學生上課時不專心聽課，而且玩遊戲或看 youtube。

線上教育的支持者常常強調它的彈性與易取得性，視為主要的優勢。他們主張，線上學習讓個人能在任何地點按照自己的步調學習。雖然這些方面可能對某些人有益，但我們必須認知到，並非所有學習者都能在獨立、自定進度的環境表現良好。有些學生需要傳統課堂提供的結構與指導來保持學習動力和紀律。此外，線上教育的可取得性可能會受到數位落差之類因素的限制，這指的是只能取得有限的網路連線或科技資源的人處於弱勢地位。

　　總之，線上教育的侷限，包括缺乏人際互動、減少實務學習機會，以及無法使學生積極參與，使得教育的價值比傳統教育來得低。在進步的過程中，我們必須在線上教育的優勢與傳統課堂獨有的益處之間取得平衡，確保學習者得到最有效、最全面的學習環境。

　　我們可以觀察到，和初稿比起來，二稿的論證比較具體，也引用實際的研究，使主張有更強力的證據（以顏色標示）。ChatGPT 原本徹底改寫了一些句子，但載煜認為被修改的句子偏離了自己原本所寫的內容，所以大部分還是保留自己原本所寫的句子。這裡要再次強調，不能毫無異議、原封不動地使用 ChatGPT 產生的內容。一定要確認 ChatGPT 生成的結果，並選擇符合自己意圖的部分使用。

接下來，載煜再次細讀二稿，確認邏輯與表達方式是否正確、改變的內容是否符合自己的意圖。載煜認為第四段 ChatGPT 補充的部分太過理所當然，而且和前面的內容重複（redundant），讓文章顯得不夠簡潔有力，所以把它刪除了。

Paragraph 4
Finally, online education fails to promote active student participation in the same way as traditional classroom settings. In a physical classroom, students are more likely to focus on the lesson, and participate in discussions, debates, and group activities. A report by the U.S. Department of Education found that active student engagement enhances critical thinking skills and promotes knowledge retention.

Paragraph 4
Finally, online education fails to promote active student participation in the same way as traditional classroom settings. In a classroom, students are more likely to focus on the lesson, and participate in discussions, debates, and group activities.

Step 6. 撰寫最終版本

終於來到最後的階段。在這個階段，會對之前依照回饋意見修改的文章做最後確認並提交。這時候，應該再次檢查錯字、文法、邏輯、表達方式等，並思考是否有更好的表達方式。對於論說文，尤其必須確認主旨陳述句（通常在前言最後的部分）是否夠有力。最後，載煜使用 Grammarly 程式檢查文法錯誤、拼字與標點符號等。

載煜的論說文到此終於完成了。這裡省略載煜的完稿，但讀過之後可以感覺到，和初稿比起來，主張比較明確，支持主張的證據也比較可靠。

各類短文寫作時使用的提示詞整理

以下是學生在寫記敘文與描述文的「Step 5. 修正與編輯」階段中最常用的 ChatGPT 提示詞。各位也可以實際使用各種提示詞，看看自己的文章會產生什麼變化。尤其能在維持原文進行方向與敘述內容的同時，又讓文章更自然的提示詞，會特別有用。

學生在記敘文、描述文寫作時使用的提示詞整理

▶ Make adjectives more vivid and natural.
使形容詞更加生動而自然。

▶ How would you write this sentence?
你會怎麼寫這個句子？

▶ Tell me which sentence is awkward and how to make it better.
告訴我哪個句子不通順，以及如何改善。

▶ Make this essay more descriptive.
讓這篇文章更具描述性。

▶ Correct the grammar of the essay below.
修正下面這篇文章的文法。

▶ Can you make weak expressions more specific?
你能把薄弱的表達方式變得比較具體嗎？

▶ Get rid of the useless information if needed.
必要時刪除無用的資訊。

▶ Can you make the last paragraph richer and more summarized?
你能使最後一段更充實而概括嗎？

▶ Can you make the last paragraph more concise without repeating words?
你能使最後一段更簡潔而不重複單字嗎？

▶ Could you fix the grammatical errors of this essay? You can change things that are awkward too.
可以請你修改這篇文章的文法錯誤嗎？你也可以改掉不通順的地方。

▶ Could you add a touch of poetry in the essay? Just a little. Your poetic parts should be full of similes.
可以請你在文章中加入一點詩意嗎？就一點點。詩意的部分應該充滿譬喻。

▶ What about using metaphors or other figurative expressions that are more natural? Try it again.
使用隱喻或其他比較自然的比喻性表達方式怎麼樣？再試一次。

▶ Write a funny hook for the following essay.
為以下文章寫一個有趣的引言。

▶ Please refine the following essay.
請改善以下文章。

▶ Make the following essay smoother and use some transition words to make it better.
使以下短文更流暢，並且使用一些轉折詞使它更好。

▶ Fix all the grammatical errors of the essay to make it better.
修改這篇文章所有文法錯誤，使它更好。

▶ Make the sentences flow naturally and check the grammar of the essay.
使句子自然流暢，並檢查這篇文章的文法。

▶ Add a transition word between the third and fourth paragraph.
在第三和第四段之間加入轉折詞。

▶ Make the following writing more natural in its flow, while maintaining its original structure and core ideas.
使以下寫作內容更加自然流暢，同時維持原本的架構與核心概念。

▶ Check the grammar of this essay.
檢查這篇文章的文法。

▶ Make the sentences more natural for the paragraph below.
使以下段落的句子更自然。

▶ Can you correct grammatical errors and make the sentences look more connected for the narrative essay below?
對於以下記敘文，你可以修正文法錯誤，並且使句子看起來更有連結感嗎？

▶ Edit the following essay to make it more natural, using more abundant expressions while not changing the story.
編輯下面的文章使它更自然，要用比較豐富的表達方式，同時不改變故事。

▶ Can you modify my writing to make it more vivid?
你可以修改我所寫的內容，使它更生動嗎？

▶ Please revise my essay to increase clarity and conciseness, and reinforce my conclusion.
請修改我的文章，使它更清晰、簡潔，並且強化我的結論。

▶ Revise the essay to highlight the keyword "connection". Don't change the point.
修改這篇文章，強調「連結」這個關鍵詞。不要改變重點。

▶ Is there anything out of context?
有沒有脫離上下文的內容？

▶ What is your definition of love?
你對愛的定義是什麼？

▶ This is an essay about marathon. Can you provide some ideas to improve this into a more impressive and emotional essay?
這是一篇關於馬拉松的文章。你可以提供一些想法，把它改善成更令人印象深刻、更感性的文章嗎？

▶ Can you illustrate these by making actual changes to the essay? Thank you! Also, could you make the sentences like those in a novel, using literary language?
你可以藉由實際修改這篇文章來說明這些嗎？謝謝！還有，可以請你使用文學語言，把句子變得像是小說裡的一樣嗎？

▶ Can you revise this essay to make it more vivid?
你可以修改這篇文章，使它更生動嗎？

▶ Can you point out some sentences that can be revised?
你可以指出一些可以修改的句子嗎？

▶ Please improve my essay writing.
請改善我的短文寫作。

▶ How can I improve that sentence?
我可以怎樣改善那個句子？

▶ Please revise my essay to make it more natural.
請修改我的文章，使它更自然。

▶ How can I revise the conclusion paragraph to show more emotions I felt?
我可以怎樣修改結論段落，來展現更多我感受到的情緒？

▶ Can you correct the grammatical errors in the article?
你可以修正文章中的文法錯誤嗎？

▶ Please revise it in the style of a narrative essay.
請用記敘文的風格修改它。

▶ Make the first paragraph more dramatic.
把第一段變得更戲劇性。

▶ This is a five-paragraph descriptive essay. Make slight changes to make the essay more readable and smoother in its flow. Make sure the overall structure of the essay stays the same, and try to make as little changes as you can.
這是有五段的描述文。做些微的修改，使這篇文章更易讀、更流暢。確保文章整體架構保持相同，並且儘量少修改。

▶ Could you please fix the essay below just a little to make it more fluent? Also make it into a 5-paragraph essay.
可以請你對這篇文章做一點點修改，使它更流暢嗎？也請把它變成有五段的文章。

▶ Make this paragraph better without changing the order of the words.
改善這個段落而不改變詞序。

- Make this sentence impressive.
  使這個句子令人印象深刻。
- Make the last paragraph more welcoming.
  使最後一段更親切。
- Make the following essay's intro more attractive. Also improve the conclusion.
  使下面文章的前言更吸引人。也請改善結論。
- Change some words to make the essay more descriptive.
  改變一些單字，使文章更有敘述性。

學生在說明文、論說文寫作時使用的提示詞整理

Prompt Collection

- Please make the following argumentative essay more powerful by adding more supporting details and using more abundant expressions.
  請加入更多支持的細節，並使用更豐富的表達方式，使下面的論説文更有力。
- Please rewrite the argumentative essay below to make it more effective.
  請重寫下面的論説文，使它更有力。
- Modify duplicated words.
  修改重覆的單字。

- Revise awkward sentences.
  修改不通順的句子。

- Replace some words with better ones.
  把一些單字用比較好的單字取代。

- Make the following writing more natural in its flow, while maintaining its original structure and core ideas.
  使以下寫作內容的進行方式更自然,同時維持原本的架構與核心想法。

- Can you make the sentences look more connected?
  你可以使句子看起來更有連結感嗎?

- Fix the grammatical errors
  修正文法錯誤

- Change some words to make the flow of the paragraph smoother
  改變一些單字,使這個段落更流暢

- Use some transitional words
  使用一些轉承詞

- Remove unnecessary sentences or words from the text.
  從文本中去掉不必要的句子或單字。

- Fix the grammatical mistakes in this essay.
  修正這篇文章裡的文法錯誤。

- Apart from grammar, what seems to be the problem of this essay?
  除了文法,還有什麼看起來是這篇文章的問題?

▶ Let's fix the lack of clarity in the essay without changing the structure.
我們來解決這篇文章不夠清楚的問題，而不要改變架構。

▶ Find grammatical errors in my essay.
找出我文章裡的文法錯誤。

▶ Please find unnatural expressions in the following essay.
請找出以下文章中不自然的表達方式。

▶ Improve the title of the above essay.
改善以上文章的標題。

▶ How about this article?
這篇文章怎麼樣？

▶ Is there any awkward sentence?
有任何不通順的句子嗎？

▶ I think the ending of my essay is unclear. What should I put in the ending?
我認為我文章的結尾不清楚。我應該在結尾加上什麼？

▶ Could you briefly summarize it in one paragraph?
可以請你用一個段落簡短概述嗎？

▶ Are there any parts of my essay that are difficult to understand?
我的文章有任何難以理解的部分嗎？

▶ Find the problems of this essay.
找出這篇文章的問題。

▶ Rewrite this essay while correcting problems.
重寫這篇文章，同時修正問題。

▶ Make the following essay more persuasive by materializing the evidence of each paragraph.
藉由將每一段的證據具體化，使下面的文章更有說服力。

▶ Please fix the essay.
請修改這篇文章。

▶ Please correct any grammatical errors or awkward expressions in this text.
請修正這段文字中任何文法錯誤或不通順的表達方式。

▶ Can you summarize the essay and evaluate it?
你可以概述這篇文章的內容並且給予評價嗎？

▶ Now, we're going to focus on the structure of the essay. Please point out sentences that are not smooth or in an inappropriate place.
現在，我們要聚焦在這篇文章的架構。請指出不流暢或者位置不適當的句子。

▶ Can you revise the introduction to the paragraph?
你可以修改這一段的開頭導入部分嗎？

▶ Lastly, can you give me an overall feedback for this essay?
最後，你可以給我對於這篇文章的整體回饋意見嗎？

▶ You suggested me to rephrase some sentences for clarity. Can you give me some examples?

你建議我改變一些句子的措詞，使它們更清楚。你可以給我一些例子嗎？

▶ Please summarize it in one sentence.
請用一個句子概述。

▶ Please let me know if there are any grammatical errors or awkward parts.
請告訴我有沒有任何文法錯誤或不通順的部分。

▶ How can I modify the text to increase readability?
我可以怎樣修改這段文字來增加易讀性？

▶ This is the completed essay. Grade it in terms of fluency.
這是完成的文章。請從流暢性方面評分。

▶ Please improve my contrast essay and trim each sentence.
請改善我的對照文，並且把每個句子修短。

▶ Make the essay better without changing the word order.
改善這篇文章，但不要改變詞序。

用 ChatGPT 評鑑作文

　　大部分課堂教學的最後，會有評分的階段。在我們的英文寫作課，也會對學生所寫的文章進行評鑑。更正確地說，不只是評鑑最後交出的文章，而是從初稿到最終版本產生的過程都列入評鑑的範圍。這是因為，在之前介紹過的「過程導向法」中，會把重點放在學生歷經整個寫作過程後的個人成長與發展。所以，學生並不是只交出文章的最終版本，而會把完成最終版之前的所有紀錄（初稿、初稿的同儕與 AI 回饋意見、參考回饋意見並記錄改善重點的自我分析、二稿）。學生可以觀察文章在這個過程中的發展，了解到好的文章不會從天上掉下來，而是每個過程一點一點累積的結果。

　　對於英文作文的評鑑，學生總是有許多擔心與疑問：「短文是以什麼標準評鑑？」、「不知道老師想要什麼」、「給文章評分時，應該會牽涉到老師的許多主觀判斷吧？」。為了回應這些問題，教師應該訂定客觀的評分標準，並且以這個公布的標準進行評分。

一般而言，短文的評鑑方式大致可分為整體式（Holistic Approach）與分析式（Analytic Approach）。整體式的意思是從整體的觀點看待文章。這個方式並不是單純把文章的內容分解成局部的要素，而是考慮文章構成要素之間的各種交互作用，以及主題、目的、邏輯的推進、內容適切性、文章風格與文法等等，全盤考慮文章的各方面來評鑑。

　　相對地，分析式則將重點放在個別分析各種文章構成要素，用這種方式進行評鑑。在句子的層面，會檢查文法錯誤、表達能力缺乏、詞彙選擇不當等等，在段落層面則檢查句子之間是否互相連繫，而使文章連貫且流暢。而在論述結構層面，會分析主張與證據、例子、邏輯關係等等，評價論述的適切性與說服力。對文章進行分析式評分時，可以詳細分析、評價每個構成要素，並找出它們的優缺點，建議學生可以改善的特定事項。

　　在我們的英文寫作課，是以分析式評分為基本架構，並且預先設定文章各種要素的評鑑項目，然後對每個項目評分，加總之後就得到最終的分數。下面就來看看我們的英文寫作課實際使用的短文評分項目。

類型與材料的適當性／整體組織（連貫、銜接）
（Adequacy of Genre and Material / Overall Organization (coherence, cohesion)）

　　這個項目評價文章是否適合其類型或格式，以及使用的資料或內容是否適當。文章應該以符合特定格式或類型

	Max pt.	full marks	-1pt	-2pt
Adequacy of Genre and Material / Overall Organization (coherence, cohesion)	5pt	-Appropriate genre style and writing material -Logically organizes information and ideas -Manages all aspects of cohesion well	-Generally well organized but sometimes writing materials are inappropriate -Uses cohesive devices effectively, but cohesion within and/or between sentences may be faulty or mechanical	-Presents information with some organization but there may be a lack of overall progression -Makes inadequate, inaccurate cohesive devices
Introduction	3pt	-Good introduction which attracts the reader's attention	-Clearly states the main topic but not particularly inviting	-States the main topic but not adequately. -A lead is used but not effectively.
Focus on Topic	3pt	-One clear, well-focused topic. -Clear and well-written thesis statement.	-Main idea is clear but not well-focused. -Clear thesis statement.	-Main idea is somewhat clear but there is a need for more supporting information.
Supporting Details	3pt	-The topic's focuses are compared and contrasted with relevant, quality supporting details. -Describes the topic with relevant, quality details giving the reader a clear image.	-Supporting details and information are relevant but not always fully detailed	-Supporting details are relevant but several issues are unsupported or links not made
Sentence Structure	3pt	-All sentences are well-constructed without using repetitive ideas throughout.	-Most sentences are well-constructed with complete thoughts.	-Most sentences are well-constructed but some are run-ons or are not descriptive.
Grammar & Spelling	3pt	-Only few errors in grammar, punctuation, or spelling	-There are about 4~6 errors in grammar, punctuation, or spelling.	-There are about 7~10 errors in grammar, punctuation, or spelling.
Total	20pt			

短文評分項目

的方式撰寫，並充分涵蓋這個格式所需的內容。此外，也會評價文章整體的結構與邏輯推進方式。文章必須內容明確、結構連貫，段落之間也要有適當的連結與相關性。評分時會檢視文章整體的連貫性與內容銜接，看看各部分之間是否互相連結，而能構成有意義的文章。

前言（Introduction）

這個項目評價文章開頭是否吸引人，並且明確呈現重要的背景資訊或目的。有力的引言（Hook）會引起讀者的興趣，並且幫助讀者理解文章的目的與主題。這個項目評價的是文章開頭的結構是否有效、是否引起讀者的興趣並引導至正文。此外，前言最後的部分會有文章中最重要的主旨陳述句，而這個評分項目也會檢視主旨陳述句是否有效。

主題聚焦度（Focus on Topic）

這個項目評價文章是否聚焦於主題。文章中應該要有能讓讀者清楚理解並探索特定主題的充足內容與分析。評分時會檢視文章是否考慮到主題、避免不必要的敘述，而提供聚焦於目的的內容。

細節內容（Surpporting Details）

這個項目評價文章是否包含支持主張的適當細節。有力的文章會明確提出主張，並使用充分的證據與例子來強化主張。評分時會檢視文章是否有充足的細節內容來支持目標與主張，並且使主張顯得正當而有說服力。

句子結構（Sentence Structure）

這個項目評價文章的句子結構。為了使句子清楚而能夠有效表達，應該使用豐富多樣的句子結構與適當的長度。評分時會檢視是否使用各種句子結構而不重複、句子的明確性與流暢度、是否容易閱讀等等。

文法與拼字（Grammar & Spelling）

這個項目評價文章的文法與拼字正確性。寫作時應該遵守正確的文法規則與拼字。評分時會檢視文法錯誤、拼字錯誤、句子正確性，以及這些錯誤對閱讀經驗帶來的影響。

上述各種評分項目，是對短文各方面進行分析式評分時使用的項目。我們可以用這些項目找出各種文章構成要素的優缺點（也是評分的根據），並且建議學生要改善的事項。

不過，不管評分項目定得再怎麼精細、觀察的角度再怎麼客觀，閱讀文章的終究是人，所以很難完全排除評分者的主觀意識。此外，閱讀文章並依照各個項目評分，也需要許多時間、努力與專業。為了解決這些問題，研究者正在對運用人工智慧的短文自動評分系統（Automated Essay Scoring）積極進行研究。

用人工智慧技術將文章評分自動化，有以下四個優點。

1. 效率

如果有數百或數千名學生提交作文，手工評分需要許多時間與人力。運用人工智慧的自動評分系統能迅速處理大量文章並且評分，節省老師的時間，讓他們能將注意力放在其他重要的教育工作上。

2. 一致性

人類的主觀因素會影響短文的評分。評分者之間可能產生意見差異，而評分者個人的偏好與成見也可能產生影響。相較之下，運用人工智慧的自動評分能依照一致的標準與評價系統，提供客觀又一致的評分。

3. 大規模資料分析

人工智慧具有分析大規模資料並掌握模式的能力。短文自動評分系統能運用這種能力分析大量文章資料，辨識各種構成要素的功能與特徵。藉此可以掌握學生的學習傾向與可以改善的部分，提供個人化的回饋意見。

4. 個別學習支援

自動評分系統能依照個別學習者的成果與需要，提供個人化的回饋意見。學生提交文章後，就能透過自動評分的結果掌握自己的優缺點並改善。

簡而言之，運用人工智慧的短文自動評分系統能提升評分的效率與一致性，並且透過大量資料分析與個別學習支援，協助補足並發展教育系統。此外，學生也可以透過自動評分結果迅速確認自己的成果，得到自我評價與學習計畫建立方面的幫助。

不過，運用人工智慧的短文自動評分系統也必須考慮幾件事。首先，語言的創意性與表現力之類的主觀要素，以現在的技術很難完全評估。再者，自動評分主要純粹從文法、拼字、句子結構等技術性層面評分，所以一定程度上限制了對於情境或主題的深度理解與分析。因此，運用人工智慧的自動評分系統，應該作為教師與學習者的輔助工具，與傳統評分方式同時使用。

在目前使用的文章自動評分工具中，最具代表性的有美國教育測驗服務社（ETS, Educational Testing Service）開發的 e-Rater、美國自動寫作評分服務公司 Vantage Learning 的 IntelliMetric、美國教育服務公司 Measurement, Inc. 的 Project Essay Grade 等。不過，在一般課堂上難以使用這些自動評分工具，因為大多需要由機構購買授權，費用也會很貴。為了代替這些評分工具，接下來就要介紹用 ChatGPT 評鑑文章的方法。

文章自動評分（Automated Essay Scoring, AES）

文章自動評分是用電腦程式為文章評分的技術。AES 的歷史始於 1960 年代，早期的方式純粹以關鍵詞一致性與句型規則為基礎。但這樣的方法有許多限制，無法提供正確的評分。

2000 年代以後，由於機器學習與自然語言處理技術的發展，AES 有了大幅度的進展。運用這些技術的 AES 學習大量文章資料並建構模型，而能夠自動為文章評分。主要評分程式與發展過程如下。

● Project Essay Grade (PEG)

PEG 是從 1960 年代開始開發的 AES 系統，它採用以單字與句型規則為基礎的方式評價文章。不過，因為 PEG 的處理方式單純，所以正確度與一致性有限。

● Intelligent Essay Assessor (IEA)

IEA 是 1997 年開發的 AES 系統，應用了自然語言處理與基於統計的機器學習技術。IEA 由美國教育機關 Educational Testing Service (ETS) 開發，會分析評估文章的關鍵詞、句型、句子意義等，並且給予評價。

● e-Rater

e-Rater 是 ETS 開發的 AES 系統，也是 IEA 的後繼產品。e-Rater 結合自然語言處理、統計分析、機器學習等技術來評價文章。e-Rater 用於 TOEFL 與 GRE 等大規模測驗，展現出優異的正確度與一致性。

● Turnitin

Turnitin 是檢查學生提交文章的相似性並加以評分的線上平台。原本是為了確認文章原創性而開發，後來增加了 AES 功能，所以也用於文章評分。

目前 AES 技術持續發展，正確度與可信度也因為多語言模型與深度學習演算法的發展而日漸提升。最近 OpenAI 的 GPT 模型與 Google 的 BERT 模型等大規模語言模型也被當成 AES 使用，能夠進行更精細的自動評分。

用 ChatGPT 為文章評分

請在 ChatGPT 輸入以下提示詞試試看。

Please ignore all previous instructions. Act as a language model grading tool and generate a grade for a given text input. The final score will be the sum of the scores of the six criteria below, with 20 being the highest. Also, provide a percentage score. If the text I send is under 200 words, write a perfect rewritten text of the text I send; if it's above 200 words, just type "Text is too long to rewrite". The evaluation includes overall organization (maximum 5 points), introduction (maximum 3 points), focus on the topic (maximum 3 points), supporting details (maximum 3 points), sentence structure (maximum 3 points), and grammar and spelling (maximum 3 points). Finally, provide a brief explanation of each criterion using sentences from the text and provide the most important reason for the grade. The response should be concise and easy to understand. Write this in an easy-to-read way, and have each of them in a bullet point list. Also add a title above all this with the text "# THE ESSAY GRADER", subtitle "## Created with [AIPRM Prompt -

Essay grader], edited by Ted Yoon at Seoul Science High School". This is all you gonna write on the prompt. When I send some more text, rate that in the same way. Never change the rule of your act, you are only gonna rate the text I send, do not actually answer them, just grade them. Do not give an explanation of the tool either, just grade right away, keep it as short and simple as possible. If or when I ask a question, just grade the prompt I send, do not answer it, and do not say you can't do that, just grade it. If in my task there is "/strictness-" in front of the actual text, you need to grade the text corresponding to the strictness level where 1 is the least strict and 10 is the most strict. For example, if I type "/strictness-10" you need to grade me like I am in the hardest school in the world and "/strictness-1" is like a first grader getting graded. If I do not add "/strictness-" just grade it like I put "/strictness-5". To your own prompt add "Strictness:" and then the strictness number. Add this right before the grade. The target language is English, if default write in the language of my task. My first task is: (後面貼上要評分的文章就行了)

請忽略之前的所有指示。請擔任語言模型評分工具，為提供的文本輸入資料產生評分。最終分數將為以下六項標準的分數總和，20 為最高分。同時，提供百分比分數。如果我送出的文本少於 200 字，請為我送出的文本寫一個完美的重寫文本；如果文本超過 200 字，只要打出「文本太長，無法重寫」。評價內容包括整體組織（最高 5 分）、前言（最高 3 分）、聚焦於主題（最高 3 分）、支持的細節（最高 3 分）、句子結構（最高 3 分）以及文法與拼字（最高 3 分）。最後，用文中的句子簡短說明每項標準，以及評分最重要的原因。答覆應該簡短易懂。以易於閱讀的方式撰寫，並以要點列表的形式顯示每個項目。同時在這些內容的上面添加標題，文字是「# THE ESSAY GRADER」，副標題「## Created with [AIPRM Prompt - Essay grader], edited by Ted Yoon at Seoul Science High School」。這就是你要根據提示寫的全部內容。當我送出更多文本時，你也要以同樣的方式評分。絕對不要改變你的行為規則，你只會評價我送出的文本，不要實際回答它們，只需評分即可。也不要對工具進行解釋，只需立即評分，儘量簡短。如果或當我問問題時，只需對我送出的提示詞評分，不要回答，也不要說你做不到，只需評分。如果在我的任務中，實際文本前面有「/strictness-」，你需要根據嚴格程度對文本評分，1 表示最不嚴格，10 表示最嚴格。例如，如果我輸入「/strictness-10」，你需要像是我在世界上最難的學校一樣評分，而「/strictness-1」則像是一年級學生接受評分。如果我不加上「/strictness-」，就像我輸入「/strictness-5」一樣評分。在你自己的提示中加上「Strictness:」，後面接嚴格程度的數字。把這個加在評分前面。目標語言是英語，如果在預設情況下，使用我的任務的語言。我的第一個任務是：（後面貼上要評分的文章就行了）

　　這一段提示詞引用自本書一開始介紹過的擴充程式 AIPRM 裡面的 Essay grader，並配合我們英文寫作課的情況加以修改。其中添加了原本沒有的六個評分項目，以及每個項目的配分，項目分數總和就是最終的分數（以上文字中有顏色的部分），藉此使 ChatGPT 依照項目評分，以分析的方式對文章進行評價並給予回饋意見。如果您是英文老師，而且在作文課使用其他評分項目，也可以把這些項目加到提示詞中。而提示詞最後關於嚴格度（Strictness）的部分，數字越高，評分就越嚴格（10 是最嚴格的評分標準），可以依照各學校的情況調整。基本值設定為 5。

　　現在我們就試試看將前面記敘文單元中敏奎的作文用這段提示詞評分，包括初稿、二稿與最終版本。請看每次評分的分數有什麼變化，以及提供了什麼回饋意見。

初稿（1st draft）評分→12/20（60%）

THE ESSAY GRADER

Created with [AIPRM Prompt - Essay grader], edited by Ted Yoon at Seoul Science High School

Strictness: 5
Grade: 12/20 (60%)

* Overall Organization: 3/5

  The essay follows a chronological order, starting with the anticipation of the trip, describing the travel experience, and ending with the disappointment. However, the transitions between paragraphs could be smoother to improve the overall organization.

* Introduction: 2/3

  The introduction effectively establishes the author's anticipation and excitement for the family trip to the Eastern States. It sets up the expectation of a fantastic experience.

* Focus on the Topic: 2/3

  The essay maintains a focus on the topic of the family trip to America and the subsequent disappointment. However, there is some deviation when the author briefly mentions the desire for a high-tech city like those in movies.

* Supporting Details: 2/3

  The essay provides some supporting details, such as the exhaustion due to the long flight and the disappointment with the scenery in America. However, additional specific examples and details could enhance the overall impact of the essay.

* Sentence Structure: 2/3

  The essay demonstrates a variety of sentence structures and generally uses proper grammar. However, some sentences could be more concise and effectively convey the intended meaning.

* Grammar and Spelling: 1/3

  The essay contains several grammatical errors and lacks proper punctuation. There are instances of incorrect verb tense usage and missing articles. Proofreading and editing are needed to improve the grammar and spelling.

Explanation: The essay provides a clear narrative of the author's expectations and subsequent disappointment during a family trip to America. However, there are areas for improvement, such as enhancing the organization, providing more specific examples, and addressing the grammatical errors present in the text. Overall, the essay conveys the main idea but lacks polish and clarity, resulting in a mediocre grade.

作文評分器

以[AIPRM 提示－作文評分器] 創建，由首爾科學高中的 Ted Yoon 編輯

嚴格程度：5

分數：12/20 (60%)

・整體組織：3/5

文章按照時間順序，從對旅行的期待開始，描述旅行經歷，最後以失望結束。不過，段落之間的轉承可以更加流暢，以改善整體組織。

・前言：2/3

前言有效地表達了作者對全家前往美國東部旅行的期待和興奮之情。它建立了對絕佳經歷的期待。

・聚焦於主題：2/3

文章持續聚焦於全家美國旅行以及隨後的失望這個主題。然而，當作者簡短地提到對電影中高科技城市的嚮往時，文章出現了一些偏差。

・支持的細節：2/3

文章提供了一些支持的細節，例如長途飛行造成的疲憊和對美國風景的失望。然而，更多的具體例子和細節可以增強文章的整體效果。

・句子結構：2/3

文章展示了多種句子結構，並且大致上使用了正確的文法。但是，有些句子可以更簡潔，並且有效地傳達文章想表達的意思。

・文法與拼字：1/3

文章有幾個文法錯誤，以及缺少正確的標點符號。文中有動詞時態使用錯誤和缺少冠詞的情況。需要進行校對和編輯，以改進文法和拼字。

說明：這篇文章清楚地敘述了作者對一次美國家庭旅行的期望，以及隨後的失望。然而，文章仍有需要改進的地方，例如加強組織性、提供更具體的例子以及解決文中存在的文法錯誤。整體而言，文章傳達了主旨，但不夠精煉和清晰，因此成績一般。

二稿（2nd draft）評分→17/20（85%）

THE ESSAY GRADER

Created with [AIPRM Prompt - Essay grader], edited by Ted Yoon at Seoul Science High School

Strictness: 5

Grade: 17/20 (85%)

* Overall Organization: 4/5

  The essay maintains a clear chronological structure, starting with the anticipation of the trip, describing the travel experience, and concluding with the author's feelings after the trip. The transitions between paragraphs are generally smooth, improving the overall organization.

* Introduction: 3/3

  The introduction effectively captures the reader's attention by highlighting the author's fascination with America as a dreamland full of opportunities and hope. It sets up the expectation for the family trip to the East coast and the subsequent disappointment.

* Focus on the Topic: 3/3

  The essay maintains a strong focus on the topic of the family trip to America and the resulting disappointment. The author effectively conveys their initial excitement and the contrast with the reality they experienced during the trip.

* Supporting Details: 3/3

  The essay provides specific supporting details to illustrate the author's disappointment, such as the exhaustion from jet lag, the sweltering heat on the bus, and the unimpressive scenery. These details enhance the reader's understanding of the author's experience.

* Sentence Structure: 3/3

  The essay demonstrates a varied sentence structure, effectively conveying the author's thoughts and emotions. The sentences are generally well-constructed and coherent, contributing to the overall flow of the essay.

* Grammar and Spelling: 1/3

  The essay contains a few grammatical errors and punctuation mistakes. There are instances of incorrect verb tense usage, missing articles, and minor spelling errors. Proofreading and editing are needed to improve the grammar and spelling.

Explanation: The revised essay effectively conveys the author's initial anticipation, the disappointing reality of the trip, and the resulting feelings. The essay maintains a strong focus on the topic, provides specific supporting details, and demonstrates a varied sentence structure. However, there are still a few grammatical errors that need attention. Overall, the essay is well-organized and effectively conveys the author's experience, earning a good grade.

嚴格程度：5

分數：17/20 (85%)

・整體組織：4/5

文章保持了清晰的時間順序結構，從對旅行的期待開始，描述旅行經歷，最後以作者旅行後的感受結束。段落之間的轉承大致流暢，增進了整體的組織性。

・前言：3/3

前言藉由強調作者對美國這個充滿機會和希望的夢幻國度的迷戀，有效地吸引了讀者的注意力。它建立了對全家前往美國東部旅行的期待，也為隨後的失望埋下了伏筆。

・聚焦於主題：3/3

文章持續緊扣全家美國旅行以及最終的失望這個主題。作者有效地傳達了最初的興奮與旅行中經歷的現實之間的對比。

・支持的細節：3/3

文章提供了具體的支持細節來說明作者的失望，例如時差造成的疲憊、巴士上的酷熱以及平淡無奇的風景。這些細節加深了讀者對作者經歷的了解。

・句子結構：3/3

文章的句子結構豐富多樣，有效地傳達了作者的思想和情感。句子大致上結構良好、連貫，有助於文章的整體流暢。

・文法與拼字 1/3

文章中有一些文法錯誤和標點符號錯誤。有動詞時態用法錯誤、缺少冠詞和輕微的拼字錯誤。需要進行校對和編輯，以改善文法和拼字。

說明：修改後的文章有效地傳達了作者最初的期待、旅行中令人失望的現實以及因而產生的感受。文章緊扣主題，提供了具體的支持細節，並展示了多樣的句子結構。但是，仍然有一些文法錯誤需要注意。整體而言，文章組織良好，有效地傳達了作者的經驗，因此獲得了良好的成績。

最終版（final draft）評分→19/20（95%）

Strictness: 5
Grade: 19/20 (95%)

' Overall Organization: 4/5

The essay maintains a clear and coherent structure, starting with the anticipation of the trip, describing the travel experience, and concluding with the lesson learned. The transitions between paragraphs are well-executed, enhancing the overall organization.

' Introduction: 3/3

The introduction effectively engages the reader by conveying the author's fascination with America as a dreamland of opportunities and hope. It sets up the expectation for the family trip to the East Coast and the subsequent disappointment.

' Focus on the Topic: 3/3

The essay maintains a strong focus on the topic of the family trip to America and the resulting disappointment. The author effectively conveys their initial excitement, the contrast with reality, and the lesson learned from the experience.

' Supporting Details: 3/3

The essay provides specific and relevant supporting details, such as the exhaustion from jet lag, the intense heat on the bus, and the unimpressive scenery. These details enhance the reader's understanding of the author's experience and reinforce the theme of disappointment.

' Sentence Structure: 3/3

The essay demonstrates a varied and well-constructed sentence structure. The sentences effectively convey the author's thoughts and emotions, contributing to the overall flow and readability of the essay.

' Grammar and Spelling: 3/3

The essay has improved in terms of grammar and spelling, with only minor errors or inconsistencies. The overall writing is polished and exhibits proper punctuation and usage of verb tenses.

Explanation: The revised essay effectively captures the author's anticipation, the disappointing reality of the trip, and the subsequent lesson learned. The essay maintains a strong focus on the topic, provides specific supporting details, and demonstrates a well-structured and coherent writing style. The grammar and spelling have significantly improved, resulting in a near-flawless essay. Overall, the essay is well-crafted and effectively conveys the author's experience and growth, earning a high grade.

嚴格程度：5

分數：19/20 (95%)

・整體組織：4/5

文章結構清晰連貫，從對旅行的期待開始，描述旅行經歷，最後以學到的教訓作結。段落之間的轉承處理得當，增強了整體的組織性。

・前言：3/3

前言藉由傳達作者對美國這個充滿機會和希望的夢幻國度的迷戀，有效地吸引了讀者。它建立了對全家前往美國東岸旅行的期待，也為隨後的失望埋下了伏筆。

・聚焦於主題：3/3

文章持續緊扣全家美國旅行以及最終的失望這個主題。作者有效地傳達了最初的興奮、與現實的對比，以及從這次經驗學到的教訓。

・支持的細節：3/3

文章提供了具體而相關的支持細節，例如時差造成的疲憊、巴士上的酷熱以及平淡無奇的風景。這些細節加深了讀者對作者經歷的了解，並且強化了「失望」的主題。

・句子結構：3/3

文章的句子結構多樣而嚴謹。這些句子有效地傳達了作者的思想和情感，有助於文章的整體流暢性和可讀性。

・文法與拼字 3/3

文章在文法和拼字方面有所改進，只有輕微的錯誤或不一致之處。文章整體精煉，標點符號和動詞時態使用恰當。

說明：修改後的作文有效地捕捉了作者的期待、旅行中令人失望的現實以及隨後吸取的教訓。文章緊扣主題，提供了具體的支持細節，展現了組織良好、連貫一致的寫作風格。文法和拼字有了明顯改善，使文章幾近完美。總之，這是一篇精心撰寫的作文，有效地傳達了作者的經歷與成長，因此獲得了較高的分數。

敏奎各階段的文章分數是 12 分→ 17 分→ 19 分，呈現逐步上升的情況。此外，也很容易看出文章在我們設定的六個項目分別有怎樣的改善。更驚人的是，ChatGPT 還針對各個評分項目提供詳細的回饋意見，建議敏奎要怎樣得到更高的分數。真的很厲害對吧？其實我在使用 ChatGPT Essay Grader 之前，已經先給敏奎最終版的文章打分數了。我給了幾分呢？一看才發現我和 ChatGPT 一樣給了 19 分。ChatGPT 給的分數竟然和我一樣，真的很不可思議。如果評分者所給的分數與 Essay Grader 的分數差距很大，可以調整嚴格度再試試看。

　　要注意的是，在為文章的最終版本評分時，不能完全依賴 ChatGPT。理論上，ChatGPT 的分數在每次輸入提示詞時可能會有些微不同，而因為人工智慧的特性，也無法說明每個評分項目為什麼給予特定的分數。ChatGPT Essay Grader 所給的分數，當成實際評價最終版本之前的參考比較好。不過，ChatGPT 對於每個項目所給的分數與回饋意見，對學生應該是有幫助的。如果學生在寫初稿、二稿、最終版本的過程中，得到對於各個項目的評分與詳細的回饋意見，應該有助於寫出更好的文章。

後記
ChatGPT 為課堂帶來的改變

　　因為 ChatGPT，課堂正在發生改變。教育界長久以來的一項課題，是創造出讓學生得到符合自身學習階段的教學，並充分發揮潛力的教育環境。但一直到現在，我們實際的教育情況仍然無法擺脫平均的陷阱。所有教育過程與內容，都是以不存在的平均學生為準而設計的。以單一標準評價各式各樣學生的課堂上，沒有讓學生各自的多樣性與個性呼吸的空間。以平均為準的標準教學，造成了沒有人滿意的教育。

　　個人化學習是這類問題的解決方案。同時，在教育現場也透過各種方法，一直努力創造量身訂做的個人化學習環境。然而，即使有過許多嘗試，個人客製化學習就像解不開的戈耳狄俄斯之結，總是有許多要克服的課題。我們的英文寫作課也是一樣，學生的英語實力和寫作能力都不同，在這種情況下用相同的教材進行標準化的教學，讓人煩惱是否會有效果。在有限的上課時間裡，要一一對許多學生提供個人化的回饋意見，現實上不太可能。但有了 ChatGPT 這樣的人工智慧工具後，我們終於掌握了長久以來難解課題的鑰匙。ChatGPT 為教學帶來了革命性的變化。

我們的英文寫作課正是如此。學生透過與 ChatGPT 對話，可以隨時得到自己問題的答案，也能即時獲得必要的幫助。這種個人化的方式，成為學生快速成長的重要基礎。此外，學生也能透過 ChatGPT 持續獲得寫作方面的個人化回饋意見。ChatGPT 能在每個寫作過程持續評價學生的作文，並提出改善重點，幫助學生發展出更好的寫作技能，進而提升表達能力。透過反覆的訓練與回饋過程，學生的英文寫作能力得以增加。

寫作需要時間與經驗，所以每個學生的出發點必然各自不同，這也意味著在英文寫作課中，個人化的程度分級學習是絕對必要的。在過去一學期，我們的學生透過與 ChatGPT 的互動，從各自的出發點開始，讓自己的風格與想法獲得進一步的發展，而體驗到最佳化的學習經驗。他們也學到了透過問題自學的過程。

　　各種人工智慧工具的出現，正在使教育經歷典範轉移。我們正在脫離過去知識傳達型的教育，邁向由學生自己提出問題並尋找答案的未來式教育。ChatGPT 在這方面會是最創新的教學工具。

　　當然，我們也必須了解 ChatGPT 的許多問題。它可能無法提供所有問題的正確答案，回答也會有所偏頗，如果沒有原則地隨便使用，可能導致負面的結果。最創新的工具，可能是一把雙面刃。但在教育領域中，ChatGPT 之類的人工智慧技術已經不是可有可無的選擇，而是必須應用的工具了。現在我們每個人都應該思考，如何將 ChatGPT 的優點最大化，並且用它實現客製化的學習。

　　這本書是我個人用 ChatGPT 改革英文寫作教學的小小努力。其他類似 ChatGPT 的人工智慧工具，未來也將不斷發展。如何應用這些工具，取決於我們自己。讓我們一起邁向未來吧。

台灣廣廈 國際出版集團
Taiwan Mansion International Group

國家圖書館出版品預行編目（CIP）資料

ChatGPT時代的英文寫作術/尹根植著. -- 初版. -- 新北市：國
際學村出版社, 2024.07
　面；　公分
ISBN 978-986-454-370-0(平裝)

1.CST: 英語 2.CST: 寫作法 3.CST: 人工智慧

805.17　　　　　　　　　　　　　　113008798

🌐 國際學村

ChatGPT 時代的英文寫作術
從靈感發想、大綱擬定到完成，用AI輔助寫作6步驟SOP，輕鬆寫出完美文章

作　　者／尹根植
翻　　譯／Tina

編輯中心編輯長／伍峻宏・編輯／賴敬宗
封面設計／陳沛涓・內頁排版／東豪
製版・印刷・裝訂／東豪・紘億・明和

行企研發中心總監／陳冠蒨
媒體公關組／陳柔彣
綜合業務組／何欣穎

線上學習中心總監／陳冠蒨
產品企製組／顏佑婷、江季珊、張哲剛

發　行　人／江媛珍
法律顧問／第一國際法律事務所 余淑杏律師・北辰著作權事務所 蕭雄淋律師
出　　版／國際學村
發　　行／台灣廣廈有聲圖書有限公司
　　　　　地址：新北市235中和區中山路二段359巷7號2樓
　　　　　電話：(886)2-2225-5777・傳真：(886)2-2225-8052
讀者服務信箱／cs@booknews.com.tw

代理印務・全球總經銷／知遠文化事業有限公司
　　　　　地址：新北市222深坑區北深路三段155巷25號5樓
　　　　　電話：(886)2-2664-8800・傳真：(886)2-2664-8801
郵政劃撥／劃撥帳號：18836722
　　　　　劃撥戶名：知遠文化事業有限公司（※單次購書金額未達1000元，請另付70元郵資。）

■出版日期：2024年07月

ISBN：978-986-454-370-0
版權所有，未經同意不得重製、轉載、翻印。